The Price to Pay
A thriller
Ian Hornby

New Theatre Publications - London
www.plays4theatre.com

The edition published in 2013

New Theatre Publications

2 Hereford Close | Warrington | Cheshire | WA1 4HR | 01925 485605

www.plays4theatre.com   email: info@plays4theatre.com

New Theatre Publications is the trading name of the publishing house that is owned by members of the Playwrights' Co-operative. This innovative project was launched on the 1st October 1997 by writers Paul Beard and Ian Hornby with the aim of encouraging the writing and promotion of the very best in New Theatre by Professional and Amateur writers for the Professional and Amateur Theatre at home and abroad.

ISBN 9 781 840 94925 4

Characters

Laura Nuttall
Roger Nuttall, *her husband*
Carol Anderson, *her friend*
Dianne
Barry
Maria Pearson, *Detective Inspector*
Dave Robinson, *Detective Sergeant*

Synopsis of scenes

The action of the play is split between the living room of the Nuttalls' semi-detached house and a room in a deserted farmhouse in the country. The time is the early 1990s

ACT I Scene 1 - *a Wednesday morning in summer*
ACT I Scene 2 - *evening, the same day*
ACT II - *the following morning*

Copyright Information

Video-Recording of Amateur Productions

Performing Licence Applications

A performing licence for these plays will be issued by "New Theatre Publications" subject to the following conditions.

Conditions

1. That the performance fee is paid in full on the date of application for a licence.
2. That the name of the author(s) is/are clearly shown in any programme or publicity material.
3. That the author(s) is/are entitled to receive two complimentary tickets to see his/her/their work in performance if they so wish.
4. That a copy of the play is purchased from New Theatre Publications for each named speaking part and a minimum of three copies purchased for backstage use.
5. That a copy of any review be forwarded to New Theatre Publications.
6. That the New Theatre Publications logo is clearly shown on any publicity material. This is available on our website.

Fees

Details of script prices and fees payable for each performance or public reading can be obtained by telephone to (+44) 01925 485605 or to the address below.

Alternatively, latest prices can be obtained from our website www.plays4theatre.com where credit/debit cards can be used for payment.

To apply for a performing licence for any play please write to New Theatre Publications 2 Hereford Close, Warrington, Cheshire WA1 4HR or email info@plays4theatre.com with the following details:-

1. Name and address of theatre company.
2. Details of venue including seating capacity.
3. Dates of proposed performance or public reading.
4. Contact telephone number for Author's complimentary tickets.

Or apply directly via our website at www.plays4theatre.com

The Price to Pay
a thriller by Ian Hornby
Cast *(in order of appearance)*

Laura Nuttall
Roger Nuttall. . . . . *Laura's husband*
Carol Anderson. . . . . *A friend*
Dianne
Barry
Maria Pearson. . . . . *A Detective Inspector*
Dave Robinson.. . . . . *A Detective Sergeant*

The action of the play is split between the living room of the Nuttalls' semi-detached house and a room in a deserted farmhouse in the country.

ACT I Scene 1. . . . . *a Wednesday morning in summer*

ACT I Scene 2. . . . . *evening, the same day*

ACT II.. . . . . *the following morning*

The Price To Pay was originally performed by the TOADS Theatre Company at the Torquay Little Theatre, with the following cast:-

Laura Nuttall.. . . . . *Alexa Tewksbury*
Roger Nuttall. . . . . *Martin Austin*
Carol Anderson. . . . . *Suzy Miles*
Dianne. . . . . *Rachel Neal*
Barry. . . . . *Mark Neal*
Maria Pearson. . . . . *Lora Grochala*
Dave Robinson.. . . . . *David Wilson*

Directed by Alec Stokes

If this play is to have its full impact it is essential that the various contrasts are highlighted. There is the immediate visual contrast of the two areas of the set - the everyday normality and simplicity of the living room against the dilapidated squalor of the farmhouse. This is amplified by the contrast between the language and behaviour in the two acting areas, gradually drawing closer as the despair and anger build up. The impact of the switches of action between the two acting areas can be made more dramatic by the use of lighting to highlight the "live" area, leaving the other area dimmed.

The play is set in the early 1990's. It should not be brought into present day, since phone-tracing techniques have advanced considerably since then and the "partial trace" idea would no longer be relevant.

Language - *To retain the characterisation in some of the situations some strong language is appropriate. It is left to the individual director to use such language as he or she sees fit and to suit their audiences and without compromising the author's discretion.*

ACT I Scene 1

The stage is split in half. Stage R is the living room of the Nuttalls' house. Above R is a door leading to the rest of the house. There is an implied "window" in the "fourth wall". The room is brightly and cleanly decorated. The room is sparingly furnished with a settee C and matching armchair R. There is a dining chair above C. Down C is a small telephone table with a modern telephone and directories. Down R is a television set. Stage L is a room in an abandoned country barn or farm building. The room contains a dirty old bed (or possibly some straw bales covered in a blanket) and a single chair or box. A door L leads to the rest of the barn. The place is very dirty and dank in complete contrast to the right of the stage. There is an implied window high in the "fourth wall". A single hanging light bulb without a shade hangs C.

As the curtain opens the "barn" is deserted. The lights are up stage R and down stage L. In the living room Laura is sitting on the settee watching morning television. She is smartly but casually dressed.

Roger   *(off R; distant)* Laura, have you seen my blue tie?

Laura   *(calling)* It's on your tie rack.

Roger   I've looked there.

Laura   Look again.

(Laura listens for a moment, but when there is no further reply she smiles and returns to her television. She flips channels idly with the remote control. Shortly footsteps are heard coming

downstairs and Roger enters R. He is hurriedly getting ready to go out to work, and carries a blue suit jacket over his arm and a briefcase. He puts the briefcase down by the telephone table.) Find it?

Roger *(sheepishly holding up the blue tie)* On my tie-rack.

Laura What would you do without me, darling?

Roger Go out and spend all the money I'd save.

Laura You don't know when you're well off.

Roger Yes, Laura. Anything you say. *(He puts on his jacket and starts looking for his car keys.)* Now what did I do with my damned keys?

Laura On the thingy in the hall, as usual.

Roger On the thingy. Right. *(He glances at his watch.)* I'd better be off. I'll be late.

Laura You've got plenty of time. Stop panicking. *(There is a knock on the back door off R.)* That'll be Carol. Let her in, will you?

Roger *(moving towards the door R)* Yes, O.K. You going out to lunch again?

Laura Yes. I did tell you.

Roger Well go easy on the money, will you? I know I get paid this week, but it's a five week month next month and...

Laura We're only going to the pub for a ploughman's... not to the Ritz.

(There is another knock at the back door.)

Roger I know, but...

Laura *(interrupting)* Will you let Carol in? She'll think we've moved away.

(Roger makes as if to speak, but thinks better of it and exits R. The back door is heard to open.)

Roger *(off R)* Morning, Carol.

Carol *(off R)* Hello, Roger. I didn't expect you to be here. You'd better be off, hadn't you? You'll be late.

(The back door is heard to close off R.)

Laura *(calling through)* He's got plenty of time!

(Carol enters R followed by Roger.)

Roger Laura thinks I've got plenty of time.

Laura I don't want him rushing. He drives like a maniac if he thinks he's late.

Carol *(sitting next to Laura)* Sorry. Didn't mean to cause a domestic.

Roger *(ready to go)* Right... I'll be off. *(He leans over and gives Laura a long kiss.)* See you later.

Laura 'Bye, darling. Don't go racing. You've got...

Roger *(interrupting)* I know... plenty of time. *(They briefly kiss again.)*

Carol You won't have if you carry on kissing all morning!

Roger *(straightening up)* Yes, 'course. Right. 'Bye, darling. 'Bye, Carol.

(Roger picks up his case on the way to the door and exits R. The front door opens and closes and during the next few lines a car is heard to start and leave.)

Carol Right pair of lovebirds, aren't you..? *How* long have you been married?

Laura Seven years.

Carol *(teasing)* Seven years! You act like it was seven days ago.

Laura *(defensive)* Well?

Carol All *I* get in the morning is a bacon-and-egg flavoured peck.

Laura Sorry. Didn't mean to embarrass you.

Carol Oh, don't get me wrong, Laura. I'm green with jealousy. We just... *(with a shrug)* take that sort of thing for granted, I suppose.

Laura Carol! That's awful.

Carol Oh, it's not so bad. *(She pauses in thought. Then, changing the subject; brighter)* Right! Where are you taking me today?

Laura I thought we'd have a ploughman's at the Ritz.

Carol The where?

Laura Just joking. Roger was going on about us being short of money, so I told him we were going for lunch at the Ritz.

Carol Things that bad?

Laura Oh, no... not really. Just me being gloomy. There's plenty worse off than us. If he could only get that promotion it'd help.

Carol Looks like no Ritz, then.

Laura Afraid not.

Carol How about the Coach and Horses, then? My treat.

Laura *(awkward)* No.., look.., when I said we were hard up.., I wasn't meaning that you should…

Carol   You can get them next time. Perhaps you'll win the pools and we'll be able to celebrate at the Ritz.

Laura   *(joking)* We can't afford to do the pools.

Carol   Why don't you go back to work?

Laura   Roger says no. He's very old fashioned about some things.

Carol   Ah, well. Look on the bright side. Something'll turn up.

Laura   Yes, I suppose you're right.

Carol   Come on, cheer up.

Laura   I've got some coffee brewing in the kitchen. Fancy one?

Carol   Mmm. Please.

(Laura stands and exits R. Carol watches television.)

Laura   *(off R)* What shall we do with the rest of the morning?

Carol   I want to do some shopping. New curtains for our bedroom.

Laura   *(as she enters carrying coffee)* Marks and Sparks have some nice ones. *(Gives a coffee to Carol and sits.)* And they've got some lovely matching duvet covers as well.

Carol   I was hoping you'd help me choose. You've got a much better eye than I have.

Laura   Flatterer!

Carol   Let's drink up and go. Even if we can't afford to buy anything we can window shop. At least that's free.

Laura   O.K. *(Glances at her watch.)* There's a train at quarter to.

Carol   *(draining her coffee)* Can I just use the loo before we go?

Laura   Help yourself.

(Carol exits R and is heard climbing the stairs. Laura watches television while sipping her coffee. There is a ring at the doorbell off R. Laura puts down her mug, stands and switches off the television, then exits R. The front door is heard to open off R. Dianne and Barry are there. Dianne talks very officiously, whereas Barry talks with a thick accent and is rather slow and ponderous.)

Dianne *(off R)* Good morning… Mrs Nuttall?

Laura   *(off R)* Yes.

Dianne Mrs *Laura* Nuttall?

Laura Yes...

Dianne I'm Inspector Collier. This is Detective Sergeant Baines.

Barry *(stiffly)* Morning, Ma'am.

Laura What is all this?

Dianne May we come in, Mrs Nuttall?

Laura Er... Well, yes.

Dianne Thank you, Mrs Nuttall. In here? *(Dianne enters R, followed by Laura and Barry.)*

Laura Now look, will you please explain...?

Dianne Your husband is Mr Roger Nuttall, who works at Glover Engineering?

Laura Yes, but what's happened?

Dianne Where he is a manager in the Administration Department?

Laura Yes, yes. Look, will you please tell me...? *(She has an awful idea.)* Has there been an accident...? Has Roger been hurt? I told him not to rush. *(frantic)* Oh, my God! Tell me!

Dianne *(to Barry)* Looks like we have the right Laura Nuttall.

Barry Looks like it. *(Slowly walks round behind Laura while she eyes them both anxiously.)*

Laura *(turning to Barry; near to tears)* Why won't you tell me?

Dianne *I'll* tell you, Mrs Nuttall.

Laura *(turning to face Dianne; desperate)* What?

Dianne *(to Barry)* Grab her, Barry!

(Barry, from his position behind Laura, puts one hand across her mouth to stop her screaming and his other arm firmly around her, grasping both arms. Laura starts to struggle.)

Barry Keep still, you cow!

Dianne Keep hold of her can't you?

Barry I'm tryin'!

Dianne I'll soon stop her. *(She takes a small bottle of liquid and a pad of cotton wool out of her bag. She pours some of the liquid on the pad and advances on the struggling Laura.)* Can't you keep her still?

Barry I'm tryin', I'm tryin'!

(Dianne takes a pistol from her bag. Laura looks in horror, but

stops struggling. Dianne points the pistol at Laura a few inches from her face.)

Dianne Now keep still, or I'll stop you struggling for good.

(Barry takes his hand from Laura's mouth. Laura gulps in breath but does not scream. Dianne pushes the pad across Laura's mouth.)

Laura *(against the pad)* No!

(There is a brief struggle before Laura goes limp in Barry's arms. Dianne keeps the pad on her mouth.)

Barry That's enough! Don't overdo it. We need her alive.

Dianne For now at least... I know what I'm doing.

Barry *(Carries the limp Laura to the settee and lays her on it. He looks at her, concerned.)* She ain't breathing. I think you've killed her!

Dianne *(going to Laura and checking her breathing)* Get stuffed, Barry. Don't be so bloody stupid. She's all right.

Barry I'll go and check the back way. We'd better get her in the van.

(The sound of a toilet flushing is heard off R.)

Dianne *(hushed)* Shit! What was that?

Barry There's somebody else here. *(Slightly panicky)* What if they heard us?

Dianne Don't be such a fool. If they'd heard us all hell'd've been let loose by now.

Barry We'd better get out of here.

Dianne No! Don't panic. *(She reaches in her bag and pulls out two ski masks.)* Here... Put this on. We might be able to turn this to our advantage.

Barry What? How?

(The sound of footsteps descending the stairs is heard off R. Dianne hands a mask to Barry and puts hers on.)

Dianne *(hushed)* Just put it on.

Barry *(puts on his mask; hushed)* Now what?

Dianne You grab whoever it is when they come in. Get behind the door.

(Barry moves behind the door while Dianne crouches behind the settee, pistol at the ready.)

Carol *(as she enters)* There we are! All ship shape and... *(In the doorway she notices Laura's inert form on the settee and starts* *towards her.)* Laura!

(Barry grabs Carol, again stopping any screaming with a hand across her mouth. Carol struggles. Dianne stands from behind the settee and points the gun at Carol's face.)

Dianne Keep still, or I'll blow your head off!

(Carol still struggles. Dianne goes to her and points the pistol at her close to her face.)

I mean it! You won't be the first I've shot.

(Carol, terrified, stops struggling.)

Good girl. Now… my… *associate* here is going to take his hand from your mouth. And you're not going to scream, are you? *(There is no reaction. Pointing the gun closer; with menace) Are you!?*

(Carol slowly shakes her head and Barry tentatively moves his hand away. Carol does not scream.)

There's a good girl! Now just keep it that way and nobody'll get hurt. O.K?

Carol All right, all right. What have you done to Laura?

Barry She's having a little sleep. We gave her some chloroform, see? She's all right… *(Suddenly menacing)* for now!

Carol But what do you want? Who are you?

Dianne Nosey cow, aren't you? I'll explain all that in a minute. You're lucky… you're going to be very useful.

Carol Why..? What..?

Dianne *(reacting)* In a minute! *(To Barry)* Go and see if you can find some rope or something.

Barry *(still holding Carol's arms)* But what about *her*?

Dianne *(holding the pistol up to Carol's face threateningly)* She'll behave, won't you, my love…? Let her go.

(Barry releases Carol's arms. Carol goes to Laura and bends over her.)

(to Barry) Now, get that rope.

Barry Right. *(He exits R.)*

Dianne *(her pistol still trained at Carol, but more relaxed)* Sit down! *(She motions Carol towards the dining chair with her pistol.)* Over there!

(Carol rises from Laura, goes to the chair and nervously sits.)

Now... who exactly are you?

Carol My... My name's Carol. I'm... I'm just a friend. We're... we were going shopping.

Dianne *(calm and motherly again)* Well, Carol, I'm afraid you'll have to call off your little shopping trip. As I said, you're going to be very useful. You can save us a telephone call.

Carol But... I don't understand.

Dianne *(with sudden venom)* You will if you'll just shut up and listen for a few minutes! *(After a moment; calm again)* That's better. Now, in case you haven't realised, we're going to take your pal Laura there on a little trip.

Carol What d'you mean...? Where..?

(Dianne advances on Carol and raises her pistol again. Carol cowers.)

Dianne *(venomous again)* Are you totally stupid? Do I have to spell it out for you?

Carol *(terrified)* I'm sorry! I don't understand! This sort of thing doesn't happen to people like us!

Dianne *(stroking Carol's cheek with the pistol)* Oh, yes it does, my sweet. Your friend here is being kidnapped.

Carol Kidnapped!? But why? Laura and Roger haven't got any money. They're broke!

Dianne It's not *their* money we're after.

Carol Then what...?

Dianne *(calling to off R)* Come on! Haven't you found anything yet?

Barry *(as he enters, carrying several ties, a scarf, etc.)* These are the best I could find. They were in a washing basket in the kitchen.

Dianne *(after a sigh; patiently)* They'll have to do. Make sure our little friend here can't cause any mischief before the man of the house returns.

(Barry ties Carol's hands behind her and her feet to the legs of the chair.)

Barry What about a gag? She'll shout the place down as soon as we go.

Carol I won't. I promise. I'll do whatever you say, only please... don't hurt us.

Dianne *(selects something suitable; to Barry)* Use this. *(hands it to him)*

(Despite her struggles, Barry gags Carol.)
I want to give Carol here a few instructions. It'll save us calling later.

Barry   Good idea.

Dianne Now, Carol. I want you to remember everything I tell you. D'you think you can? *(Carol nods.)* Good. You'd better, because your friend's life depends on it. Don't forget that, will you? *(Carol shakes her head.)*

Barry   Shall I rip out the phone…? In case she gets free?

Dianne Don't be stupid! They'll need it. *(She checks Carol's bonds.)* Anyway, Carol isn't going anywhere.

Barry   Right. I'll go and get the van round the back. *(He exits R.)*

Dianne Now… I want you to tell Roger *everything* I tell you. I won't tell you "No Police" because I know it wouldn't do any good. So tell him to go ahead and call the stupid bastards. *(Sneering) They'll* never find *us* in a month of Sundays. But warn him - if the police come anywhere near us his darling little wife there ends up dead. Got that?

(Carol nods.)

Next… We'll be in touch by phone. Tell him to stay off work - he can say he's ill, or something - and we'll phone him with instructions. If he does *exactly* as we say then he'll get his pretty little wife back safe and sound. One false step and he'd better get out his insurance policies. O.K..? Oh, and tell him… it *won't* be quick!

Barry   *(as he enters R.)* The van's round the back.

Dianne Right, We'll be off. *(With sadistic humour)* Don't go away, will you?*(Back to business; to Barry, indicating Laura)* Bring her!

(Barry lifts the inert Laura off the sofa and carries her out R. Dianne follows.)

(To Carol, as they exit) Goodbye, now. Don't forget to tell Roger we called. *(She chuckles to herself as she exits.)*

(The back door is heard to open and close and there is silence. Carol's shouts for help just come out as a mumble against her gag as she struggles to free herself. A van is heard to pull away off. The curtain slowly closes.)

ACT I Scene 2

Evening of the same day. The scene is the same as at the end of Scene 1, with stage L dim and stage R bright. Carol is still bound in the chair, but looks rather more dishevelled from struggling. The lights dim slightly stage R. Noises of a van drawing up, followed by the van doors opening and closing are heard off L. The lights come up stage L. A door is heard to open off L, and after a moment Dianne enters L, followed by Barry, who is carrying the still unconscious Laura. They are wearing the same clothes, but have taken off their ski masks.

Dianne Put her on the bed.

Barry *(carries Laura to the bed and lays her on it. He kneels and looks at her with concern.)* She's still out. How much of that stuff did you give her?

Dianne Stop worrying. She'll come round.

Barry She better had. We need her. Without her we ain't got nothing.

Dianne I told you, she'll be O.K.

Barry If she don't come round it's murder.

Dianne *(rounds on him)* It's only a problem if we're caught, and *I* don't intend to *get* caught. Stop worrying. Even if she didn't come round we can still do it without her. Her darling hubby won't know she's dead, will he?

Barry He might want to speak to her - make sure she's still alive.

Dianne *(as if talking to a child)* Well he won't be able to, will he? Anyway, I told you... she's not dead.

Barry If she does die it'll be down to you. *I'm* not getting put away for murder.

Dianne Doesn't bother *me*, Barry. Not *my* first offence, remember? It'd be life either way.

Barry Well I'm clean, so leave me out of it.

Dianne Won't make any difference in the end, will it?

Barry What d'you mean?

Dianne She dies now... or she dies later. What's the difference?

Barry Now, look, Di... I never said nothing about killing her...

Dianne Oh, piss off, Barry, you stupid bastard.

Barry *(reacts)* I ain't stupid!

Dianne She's seen us. She could pick us out. We've got no choice. She has to go.

Barry We'll be out of the Country by then, so what's it matter?

Dianne Never heard of Interpol, Barry? *(No reply.)* She dies.

Barry *(sulky)* You never said we'd have to kill her.

Dianne I never said 'cause I never thought you'd be stupid enough to think anything else.

Barry I don't like it.

Dianne I don't give a toss whether you like it or not. Once we've finished with her, she dies... Right? *(No reply. Insistent)* Right, Barry?

Barry *(reluctantly)* Yeah, I s'pose so.

Dianne Anyone'd think you had a soft spot for the cow.

Barry She's all right.

Dianne *(taunting)* You fancy her, don't you...? Go on, admit it.

Barry *(embarrassed)* No..., 'course not.

Dianne Hah! She's too good for you, my love. She'd spit in your face. But if you want to give her one, go ahead. I'm not the jealous type. Best of luck. *(She gives a derisory laugh.)*

Barry *(threatening)* Don't take the piss, Dianne. I don't like it.

Dianne *(faces up to him)* Ask me if I care. Go on, try your luck. She can hardly run away, can she? Now stop being so bloody stupid and tie her up. Make it good and tight. That little bitch is a fighter.

Barry *(takes off his tie and ties Laura's wrists behind her back)* She can't go nowhere, can she? The door's got bolts on the outside and the window's got bars.

Dianne She could scratch your shifty eyes out, though, given half a chance.

Barry *(finishes)* There. That should stop her from doing any harm.

Dianne Right. Let's eat. *(They move towards the door.)*

Barry What about her?

Dianne This ain't no 'otel, Barry.

Barry We'll have to feed her!

Dianne *(resigned)* All right... we'll bring her something back later. She can't exactly eat much like that, anyway, can she? *(Takes some keys from her pocket and throws them to Barry.)* Let's go and have a drink first. Come on... you drive.

(Barry and Dianne exit L. There are sounds of heavy bolts being closed behind the L door, then the sounds of the van doors

opening and closing and the van pulling away. After some moments the sound of a key in the front door R. The door opens and closes off R. Carol renews her struggle to get free and tries to shout but cannot.)

Roger   *(calling, from off R)* Darling! I'm home. *(Pause)* Laura! Are you upstairs? Laura…? *(After a pause, Roger enters R. He doesn't see Carol for a moment, then when he does he registers shock and hurries to her.)* Carol! What the hell's going on?

(Carol mutters against the gag. Roger takes off the gag and starts to untie her hands.)

Carol   Roger, thank God! They've taken her!

Roger   *(stops what he is doing)* What!? Who? Who has?

Carol   *(frantic)* Laura! Two people came. They've taken Laura!

Roger   Taken her?

Carol   They've kidnapped her!

Roger   My God! But… but… why? What did they want?

Carol   They left instructions for you.

Roger   But why would anyone take Laura?

Carol   Untie me, please, Roger. We must get the Police.

Roger   *(untying her hands)* No, we can't risk the Police. What if…? *(He shakes his head in disbelief.)*

Carol   But they said you *should* call the Police.

Roger   They what!? Carol, tell me exactly what they said. Everything.

Carol   They said to go ahead and call the police, 'cause the Police would never find them. Then they said if the Police come anywhere near them they'd… they'd…

Roger   What?

Carol   They said they'd kill her.

Roger   But what did they want? We haven't got any money. Why would anyone take Laura?

Carol   *(unties her feet and rubs the circulation back)* I told them that. They said they weren't after your money.

Roger   *(disbelief)* This can't be happening.

Carol   I know. I've been stuck in that chair all day. I kept telling myself the same thing.

Roger   When did it happen?

Carol They came just after you left.

Roger And you've been here all day? Was Laura... Was she all right?

Carol They'd drugged her. Chloroform, they said. She was out cold.

Roger *(suddenly angry)* If they hurt her, I'll... I'll... *(Breaks down.)* Oh God, Carol. What am I going to do?

Carol *(comforting)* It'll be all right, Roger. They said if you did what they wanted they wouldn't hurt her.

Roger If only I knew they meant that.

Carol You've got to believe it, Roger. Anything else and you'll go out of your mind. You must have hope.

Roger Hope.

Carol They obviously want her for something.

Roger But what?

Carol I don't know. They didn't say.

Roger Did you see them?

Carol What? What d'you mean?

Roger Could you describe them to the Police?

Carol No... they had ski masks on.

Roger Damn!

Carol They said they'd be in touch by telephone. You've got to stay off work and they'll phone you with instructions.

Roger When's the first call?

Carol They didn't say.

Roger I just don't believe it.

Carol You'd better get on to the Police.

Roger Yes, of course. *(Pause.)* Are you *sure* they said I should? You must have been scared stiff.

Carol I was, but I'll never forget that woman's words.

Roger Woman!?

Carol Yes, it was a man and a woman. I've been going over what they said in my mind all day, so I wouldn't forget it. Now phone the Police.

Roger *(goes to the phone and dials 999; waits for answer; into the receiver)* Police, please... Roger Nuttall... 797 0611... Yes... Please hurry... *(Impatiently)* Come on, come on... Hello, yes,

that's right... it's my wife, she's been... *(chokes on his words.)*
She's been kidnapped... What...? *(Furious)* Yes, of course I'm
bloody sure! They left her friend here with all the instructions...
All right, all right... 167 Fairview Avenue... Yes... Please hurry.
(Replaces the receiver.) They're sending someone over.

Carol Did they say how long?

Roger Straight away, they said.

Carol So we just have to wait?

Roger *(annoyed)* D'you know, they asked me if I was sure she'd been
abducted? What the hell do they think I rang them for!?

Carol They have to check, Roger. I bet they get all sorts of calls from
people whose wives are late back from the shops, or have
walked out on them.

Roger Not Laura and me.

Carol *They* don't know that.

Roger No, I suppose not.

*(They fall silent, Roger staring into his hands trying to take
everything in and Carol looking on, concerned. On the bed,
Laura stirs awake. She realises she is unable to move her arms
and gradually remembers what happened. She struggles to a
sitting position and looks around, goes to the door, listens, then,
hearing nothing, tries the handle. The door does not open. She
kicks on the door.)*

Laura *(shouting)* Hey! Let me out! Whoever you are, let me out. *(She
listens again.)* Help! Let me out! Please! *(She kicks the door
again.)* Help me! Please, somebody help me! *(She moves from
the door towards the "window".)* Where am I? Hello! Is there
anybody out there? Help me! Please, someone. *(She struggles
to try to free her hands, but cannot. She goes back to the door
and kicks on it again.)* Help me! Let me out! Please! *(more
desperate)* Is anyone there? Please, someone, help me! *(She
trails off and sinks to the floor in desperation. She sobs)*
Someone... please help me.

Roger *(glancing at his watch)* What the hell's keeping them?

Carol It's only been a fifteen minutes, Roger. Give them a chance.

Roger *(bitter)* Nobody gave Laura a chance, did they? I bet they're all
out catching bloody motorists!

Carol They'll be here. *(A car is heard to draw up fast. Carol jumps up
and runs out of the door R.)* I think it's them - the police.

Roger   Thank God. About bloody time!

(The front door is heard to open off R.)

Maria   I'm looking for Mr Nuttall.

Carol   That's right. He's in there. Come in.

Maria   Thanks. In here?

Carol   Yes. Go through.

(Maria PEARSON enters R, followed by Dave ROBINSON and Carol. Maria wears a grey skirt suit and Dave wears a dark blue suit.)

Maria   Mr Nuttall?

Roger   Yes, that's right.

Maria   I'm Detective Inspector Pearson. This is DS Robinson.

Dave   How d'you do, sir.

Maria   *(to Carol)* And you are...?

Carol   Carol Anderson. I'm Laura's friend.

Maria   Laura?

Roger   My wife. Look, can we get on with this? She... she might be...

Maria   *(calming)* All right, Mr Nuttall. We'll have to get some details from you first. We can't just go rushing off round the country chasing criminals without knowing what we're after, can we?

Roger   No, I suppose not. You'd better sit down.

Maria   *(sitting in the armchair)* Thank you, sir.

Roger   *(offering a seat with a wave of his hand)* Sergeant?

Dave   I prefer to stand, thank you, sir.

(Carol sits on the settee.)

Maria   Take notes, please, Sergeant.

Dave   *(with just a hint of disrespect)* Yes, Ma'am. *(He takes out a notebook and pen from his pocket and takes notes over the next lines.)*

Maria   Now, Mr Nuttall, can I have your full name, please?

Roger   Roger James Nuttall.

Maria   And your wife's name?

Roger   Laura Helen Nuttall.

Maria   What was her maiden name?

Roger   What the hell d'you want that for?

Maria   There are records we can search, sir.

Roger   For God's sake… she's been kidnapped! She was taken *today*, from this house, not before we were married!

Maria   Please, sir.

Roger   Baker. Laura Baker.

Maria   How old is your wife, sir?

Roger   Thirty-five.

Maria   And you, sir?

Roger   *(with a resigned sigh)* Forty.

Maria   How long have you been married, Mr Nuttall?

Roger   Seven years.

Maria   Your first marriage?

Roger   Yes… *And* Laura's.

Maria   Excuse me for asking, sir, but was it a happy marriage?

Roger   *(annoyed)* Yes, it was…! And it still *is*!

Maria   Did you and Mrs Nuttall… argue this morning?

Roger   Argue…? No, of course not, we never… *(He suddenly realises where she is leading. Furious)* Wait a minute! You don't believe me, do you?

Maria   Now, Mr Nuttall, I didn't say that.

Roger   You think we've had a fight and she's left me, don't you!?

Maria   We do get quite a lot of crank calls…

Roger   Crank..!? *Crank..!?* How dare you!?

Maria   Er… An unfortunate term, sir.., but you must understand we do get a lot of *claims* from people that their wives or husbands have gone missing and it turns out to be a marital squabble.

Roger   Will you listen to me!? She was *taken*..! From *this* house… this *morning*. Carol was a witness! They left her tied to that chair all day, for God's sake! They *threatened* her with a gun.

Maria   A witness!? Why didn't you tell us when you phoned?

Roger   I never thought you wouldn't believe me!

Dave   If *I* might be permitted, Ma'am?

Maria   *(cutting him dead)* No, Sergeant, leave this to me. Look, Mr Nuttall, we seem to have got off on the wrong footing.

Roger   Amen to that!

Maria   I'm sorry for that. This job makes you a bit blasé at times. You see so many crimes you can be a bit insensitive to the unfortunate victims.

Roger   Well *I* don't see many crimes. It's my wife we're talking about. She's gone! I want her back, Inspector.

Maria   Yes, sir… Can we start again?

Roger   Yes, I think we'd better.

Maria   *(to Carol)* You say you were a witness, Mrs Anderson?

Carol   Yes. I came downstairs and they were here. I saw Laura lying there and then they grabbed me.

Maria   How many were there?

Roger   Two. A man and a woman.

Maria   If you'd let Mrs Anderson answer, Mr Nuttall.

Roger   But she told me they…

Maria   *(interrupting)* Yes, sir, I'm sure she did, but we might just pick up on something you might have missed.

Roger   Very well.

Maria   *(to Carol)* Is that correct, Ma'am? A man and a woman?

Carol   That's right.

Maria   Are you sure there was no-one else?

Carol   No. Just the two of them.

Maria   Nobody outside? Waiting in a car, for example?

Carol   I don't think so. The man went to get the car, so I assumed… I suppose it is possible there was someone else, but the man and the woman were all I saw.

Maria   Could you describe them? Tell their ages?

Carol   Well, the man was tall. Over six feet, I'd guess…, quite big, and *very* strong. Probaby about forty.

Maria   And the woman?

Carol   Medium height and weight… average, really. Younger.

Maria   What about their faces? *(She and Dave exchange a nervous glance.)*

Carol   I didn't see their faces. They were wearing those balaclava-things with holes for their eyes.

Maria Ski masks?

Carol That's right.

Maria *(gives a relieved glance at Dave.)* Well, that's a relief, anyway.

Roger What d'you mean?

Maria Experience has shown us that in cases of kidnap where the kidnappers don't bother to disguise themselves from their victim or cover their faces they don't intend to release them. The fact that they didn't allow your wife to see their faces almost certainly means they intend to keep her alive.

Roger Thank God for that!

Dave May I, Ma'am?

Maria *(reluctantly)* Go ahead, Sergeant.

Dave Do you live locally, Mrs Anderson?

Carol Yes, four doors down. *(She indicates with her hand.)*

Dave Married?

Carol Yes.

Dave Is your husband at home, ma'am?

Carol No... he's away. He's a salesman.

Dave When will he be back?

Carol Tonight, probably. Look, what has this got to do with Laura?

Dave *(ignoring her; thoughtful; he makes a note)* I see. *(A pause.)* Would you say you are familiar with the daily comings and goings in the Avenue, ma'am?

Carol Yes, I suppose so. As much as anyone.

Dave And therefore you might be expected to notice anything out of the ordinary?

Carol I doubt it. I'm not very observant.

Maria You'd be surprised what people - especially women - notice without even realising it.

Carol Well, I'm sorry. I can't think of anything.

Dave *(to Roger)* How about you, sir?

Roger No. Not that I can think of.

Maria Perhaps if anything does come to mind you'll let us know?

Carol Yes, of course we will.

Roger Yes.

Maria *(to Roger)* I'd like to ask you about your financial...

Dave *(interrupting)* If I may be allowed to continue with my line of questions, Ma'am? *(Maria gives Dave an icy stare, but indicates for him to carry on. To Carol)* What time did you arrive at the house this morning?

Carol About quarter to nine, I suppose.

Dave Did you notice anyone hanging about outside? Perhaps someone who might fit the descriptions you gave us?

Carol No, I don't think so. I came in round the back.

Dave Think carefully, Ma'am.

Carol I can't think of anyone.

Dave What about cars? Were there any people just sitting in cars nearby, or cars you didn't recognise?

Carol No, I'm not very good with cars.

Dave *(to Roger)* You, sir? *(Roger shakes his head dejectedly.)* Did you hear the kidnappers' car leave, Mrs Anderson?

Carol Yes. They'd brought it round the back. *(shudders at the memory)* I... thought she was going to kill me... I fainted, but as I came to I heard them drive off.

Dave Was there anything specific about the sound of their car?

Carol I don't think so. I think it was probably quite old.

Dave What makes you say that, Ma'am?

Carol Well, it was quite loud, like old cars sometimes are. Rough-sounding.

Dave Did it sound anything like a taxi, for example?

Carol Yes, now you mention it, I suppose it was a bit like that. And sort of... laboured, if you know what I mean.

Dave *(making notes)* A diesel then. Possibly a van. That would enable them to drive around with Mrs Nuttall in the back without her being seen.

Carol Yes! I remember! The man said he brought the van round the back!

Dave Good! Now we know that, think back to what I was asking before... Did either of you notice any vans in the Avenue this morning?

Carol *(pensive)* I think I might have done. Over the road, farther down from here. A big blue one. Light blue. And it had patches of dark red paint on it.

Dave That'd be primer. So it's probably quite old. Have you any idea what type of van it was?

Carol No. I'm afraid not.

Dave Was it bigger than a car?

Carol Yes. Much bigger. It was a bit like the ones you have. Sort of Land Rover size.

Dave Probably a Transit or a Sherpa. Was there anything written on the side?

Carol No, I don't think so.

Dave Anyone *in* the van?

Carol Not that I noticed.

Dave And it was facing which way?

Carol Left. Towards the main road.

Dave So they possibly came from the right. Where does that lead?

Roger Out into the countryside.

Dave Can you think which way they drove off?

Carol The other way, I'd guess, but they'd driven down the lane at the back of the houses, so I don't see that proves anything.

Maria I don't suppose you happened to notice the registration number of the van?

(Dave gives a look of despair.)

Carol No. It's not the sort of thing I'd look at.

Maria Just a chance. People occasionally do.

Dave *(to Maria; slightly self-satisfied)* So, Ma'am, I've discovered it was a light blue diesel van, probably quite old, with distinguishing paint marks. And it probably headed off towards the countryside.

Maria *(aware of his attitude)* Very good, Sergeant. *(With slight disdain)* All we have to do now is find it!

Dave What did the kidnappers say?

Carol They said we should go ahead and call the police. *(in response to a quizzical look from the police)* They seemed to think you wouldn't be able find them.

Dave Confident bastards, aren't they?

Carol   They said if the police went anywhere near them they'd kill Laura.

Maria   *(attempting to comfort Roger)* Normal bravado, Mr Nuttall. Nothing to worry about in itself.

Roger   *(sarcastic)* You're a great comfort.

Maria   You'd better organise a 'phone tap, Sergeant. Call it in from the car.

Dave   *(after a sigh)* Yes, Ma'am. *(Exits R.)*

Maria   Did they give any indication of what they want?

Carol   No. All they said was that they didn't want money.

Maria   *(to Carol)* Try and remember *exactly* what they said. Did they say they didn't want money, or that they didn't want *Mr and Mrs Nuttall's* money?

Carol   *(thinking)* I... I'm not sure. They *could* have said that.

Roger   They can't want *our* money... we haven't got any. We don't own anything apart from the house, and *that's* mortgaged to the hilt.

Maria   And Mrs Nuttall?

Roger   Same as me.

Maria   Are any of your relatives wealthy?

Roger   No. We're just ordinary, everyday people.

Maria   So we *may* be able to rule out money as the motive. Unless they may mean someone else's money.

Roger   Surely they must know *we've* got no money. They seem to be very well prepared.

Maria   We're missing something. Nobody gets kidnapped for no reason. It's usually financial or political. Your wife has no political ties, I suppose?

Roger   No, none at all... Unless... Perhaps they've got the wrong woman. Perhaps they think Laura's someone else.

Maria   Possible, but unlikely. As you said, they seem to be very sure of what they're doing.

Roger   Then what, for God's sake?

Dave   *(as he enters)* The recorder's organised, Ma'am.

Maria   Thank you, Sergeant. When?

Dave   They're bringing it round straight away. They're sending it in an unmarked car in case the house is being watched.

Roger   Is that likely?

Maria   I doubt it, but better safe than sorry.

Roger   Yes, for God's sake don't take any risks.

Maria   We won't, Mr Nuttall.

Roger   Does it take long to wire up?

Dave   No, sir. Just plugs straight into your phone socket. It's not really a tap, it's just a recorder and extension phone so we can listen in. We don't need a court order to fit it, only your permission, and I assume you...?

Roger   Of course. Go ahead.

Dave   Now, where were we?

Maria   *(to Dave)* We still haven't found a motive, Sergeant. Any ideas?

Dave   *(surprised at being asked; to Roger)* What d'you do for a living, Mr Nuttall?

Roger   I'm a manager in an engineering factory.

Dave   What sort of engineering?

Roger   Electronics.

Dave   *(suddenly interested; with a glance at Maria)* Really? What sort of electronics? Any defence work, that type of thing?

Roger   No, it's all commercial stuff. Nothing sensitive. There's nothing new or secret about them. We just assemble them under licence from Japan.

Maria   That's a blind, then. It looks as though we'll just have to wait for them to get in touch.

Roger   Isn't there *anything* you can do?

Maria   Not until we know what we're dealing with, Mr Nuttall. We'll just have to be patient.

Roger   *(exasperated)* Patient!

Dave   Records can check if there's been any similar cases, Ma'am. Might at least give us some clues.

Roger   Well, for God's sake do *something*.

Maria   Good idea, Sergeant. Get on it, will you?

Dave   Already in hand, Ma'am. I took the liberty when I called in about the recorder.

Maria   *(controlling herself)* Thank you, Sergeant.

Roger   I need a drink.

Maria   That won't help, sir.

Roger   I don't care whether you think it'll help or not, Inspector.

Maria   Believe me, sir, I know how you feel.

Roger   *(exasperated)* You know how I feel? How the hell can *you* know how *I* feel...? Are *you* married?

Maria   Yes, sir, I...

Roger   And has your husband ever been kidnapped?

Maria   No, sir, but I have had experience of this sort of thing...

Carol   *(to Maria; annoyed)* Leave him alone, can't you!? *(to Roger; calming)* D'you want me to get you one?

Roger   *(hushed, to Carol)* No, I'll get it. I need a breath of air. Get away from these two.

Maria   Don't go too far away, Mr Nuttall. The telephone... they may call.

Carol   *(ushering him out of the door R)* You get your drink and sit outside. I'll come and get you if they call. *(Roger exits R. Carol closes the door behind him, then rounds on them in rage)* Just what the hell do you two think you're playing at?

Maria   *(puzzled)* I'm sorry, Ma'am?

Carol   I don't know what sort of personal vendetta you two have got between you, but whatever it is, leave us out of it, will you?

Dave   Vendetta, Ma'am?

Maria   I don't know what you're talking about.

Carol   *(in full swing)* Oh, don't you? Ever since you two arrived you've had a dig at each other every chance you get. I don't want to know why, I just want you to stop.

Dave   *(with authority)* Now look here, Mrs Anderson...

Carol   No, *you* look here, Sergeant. You were called here because *my* best friend and that poor man's wife has been kidnapped. *(getting hysterical)* And what have you done? Nothing! That's what you've done. Absolutely nothing!

Maria   We're doing everything we can, Ma'am.

Carol   Well it's not enough. I don't know what *I* can do about it, but I'll do anything to save Laura - anything. And if that means going over your heads, that's what I'll do.

Maria   Of course, Ma'am, you have a perfect right to...

Carol   *(really shouting)* I *know* I have a perfect right. But unlike you, I'm not interested in rights and wrongs. I want my friend back. I want for Roger and Laura to be together again. And that's *your* job. So why the hell don't you stop fighting and bloody-well get on with it!? *(Her outburst leaves the room in stunned silence. She is breathing hard and gradually calms down.)* Now, I'm going to see if Roger's all right. When I come back I shall want to know whether or not to make that call. *(exits R.)*

Dave   *(following her to the door R)* Of all the bloody nerve!

Maria   *(after a thoughtful pause)* No, Sergeant. She's right, you know.

Dave   *(surprised)* Ma'am?

Maria   About you and me... I know you resent me, Sergeant. There's no need to deny it. You've made everybody perfectly well aware of your opinions of me. You don't think I can handle this case, do you, Sergeant?

Dave   Off the record, Ma'am?

Maria   Off the record.

Dave   No, Ma'am.

Maria   *(frosty)* May I ask you why?

Dave   Well, Ma'am... They can teach the theory of cases like this till they're blue in the face, but every one's different, you see. No matter what they teach, you don't know which way these nutters are going to jump.

Maria   All right. Let's say for a moment I don't know how to handle it. What would *you* do that's so different?

Dave   *(unsure)* Well, Ma'am, I...

Maria   *(attacking)* Come on, Sergeant. What would *you* do if you were in charge?

Dave   A phone recorder, Ma'am.

Maria   We've organised that. It's standard procedure. What else?

Dave   Ask the locals if they saw anything.

Maria   We've done that, too.

Dave   With respect, Ma'am, we've only asked the husband and the friend. We should ask the neighbours.

Maria   True. That's a job for the uniforms. Call that in, will you? Now, what else? What ideas have *you* got that *I* haven't?

Dave   None, as yet, Ma'am. We'll have to wait until they contact the husband.

Maria In other words, you wouldn't have done anything different?

Dave Not yet, Ma'am, no.

Maria Then if you have nothing constructive to offer you should not criticise.

Dave No, Ma'am.

Maria She *was* right, though. We are letting our mutual dislike of one another get in the way. And that is unprofessional, unproductive and unforgivable.

Dave Yes, Ma'am.

Maria The truth is you resent working for a woman, don't you, Sergeant?

Dave I believe cases like this should be left to the men, yes, Ma'am.

Maria *(standing; emphasising the word "sergeant" to make her point clear)* Well.., *Sergeant* Robinson, let me make this quite clear. *I* am in charge of this case and I'm going to do the best I can for those people. Our first priority is to ensure the continued safety and subsequent return of Mrs Nuttall. Secondly - and I *mean* secondly - we shall try to apprehend the culprits. I'll do it with or without your co-operation.., *Sergeant*.., but I'd prefer to take advantage of your experience.

Dave Yes, Ma'am, but…

Maria Let me finish, Sergeant. If and when we conclude this case, any credit - *or* blame - that's going will be shared by you *and* me. We *could* make a good team, you and I. We just need to put our prejudices aside and get on with what we're paid to do. Now… are you with me or against me?

Dave With you Ma'am. For the time being at least. You're talking sense.

Maria Thank you, Sergeant.

Dave *(reluctant to apologise)* And… I'm… sorry, Ma'am. It won't happen again.

Maria I'm glad to hear it.

Dave So what about *Mr* Anderson, Ma'am?

Maria *(puzzled)* The husband…? What about him?

Dave Think he's involved? We've only her word he's away.

Maria Why should *he* be involved?

Dave   We have to explore all possibilities.

Maria   I think you're grasping at straws, sergeant. What motive could…?

(Maria stops abruptly as Roger and Carol enter R. Roger carries a glass of whisky.)

Carol   *(to Maria; with meaning)* Everything all right now?

Maria   *(to Carol)* Yes, Ma'am. All sorted. *(to Roger)* Have you a photograph of your wife, sir? Preferably a recent one?

Roger   Yes, there's one by the side of the bed.

Maria   Can you get it for us? And I'd like to see round the rest of the house if you'll allow me.

Roger   What the hell for? *(Suddenly suspicious)* You don't think that I…?

Maria   *(quickly)* I don't *think* anything, sir. I'd just like to look around. There may be some hint of who these kidnappers are, or they may have dropped something. Sergeant Robinson will check the downstairs rooms as well, if that's all right, Mr Nuttall?

Roger   Very well. *(He steps towards the door R.)*

Dave   Were the kidnappers wearing gloves, Mrs Anderson?

Carol   I'm not sure… I don't *think* so.

Dave   Good. You haven't touched anything, have you, sir? Or you, Ma'am?

Roger   Because of fingerprints, you mean?

Dave   That's right, sir.

Roger   I probably touched the door handles on the way in… And the phone, of course. But our fingerprints'll be all over the place.

Dave   Yes, sir, but we don't want to smudge any new ones, do we?

Roger   No, of course not.

Maria   Now, sir. About that photograph?

Roger   Yes. This way. *(He moves to the door R and exits.)*

Maria   *(calling after Roger)* I'll catch up with you in a moment, sir. *(to Carol)* Perhaps you'd like to have a talk with Sergeant Robinson, Mrs Anderson, while Mr Nuttall's out of the room.

Carol   But you don't suspect…?

Maria   No, Mrs Anderson. We don't suspect anything. It's merely that you might mention something that would be painful to Mr Nuttall.

I think he's had enough for the moment, don't you?

Carol   Yes, 'course. Sorry.

Maria   I'll give you as long as I can, Sergeant. Try and find out any details you can about the villains... names or places they might have said, any physical details and so on.

Dave   *(without any respect)* With respect, Ma'am, I've been on the force for a few years now. I *am* aware of procedures.

Maria   Yes, Sergeant. Of course you are. Carry on. *(She exits R; calling)* Mr Nuttall?

Roger   *(off R; distant)* Up here, Inspector.

Carol   You don't like her, do you, Sergeant?

Dave   What gives you that idea, Mrs Anderson?

Carol   You hardly hide it, do you?

Dave   Is it that obvious?

Carol   Yes, it is. What have you got against her?

Dave   I suppose she's not so bad, really. She's one of these "accelerated promotion" merchants. Straight out of University, and in ten minutes she's a D.I.

Carol   And you don't like that?

Dave   No, Ma'am.

Carol   Sounds like a case of sour grapes to me.

Dave   It may sound that way, Ma'am, but you just think for a minute... What experience has she got? They can teach in classrooms 'till they're blue in the face, but they can't teach what it's like out here.

Carol   Whereas *you* know.

Dave   I learned the hard way, Mrs Anderson. I've seen what it's like. I've seen the battered bodies, I've dragged poor sods out of crashed cars. I've seen what people can do to each other.

Carol   And she hasn't?

Dave   This is her first real case. I wouldn't like... *(He stops.)* No, Ma'am. I shouldn't be telling you all this.

Carol   No, you probably shouldn't, but I think, in the circumstances, we have a right to know. My best friend's life is on the line, here... So *what* wouldn't you like, Sergeant?

Dave   I was going to say... you mustn't repeat this. She'd have my guts for garters.

Carol   I won't.

Dave   I was going to say that I wouldn't like to be in Mrs Nuttall's shoes.

Carol   Nor I, but… *(What he has said sinks in.)* You mean you don't think she can handle the case!?

Dave   That's all I'm going to say, Ma'am. I just don't want any harm to come to Mrs Nuttall. You may be well-advised to have a word with the Chief Inspector. Kidnap cases should have specialist negotiators on them.

Carol   Thank you, Sergeant. I'll have a word with Mr Nuttall after you go.

Dave   She's doing things the wrong way round. By the book. She wants to catch these villains so she can take all the credit. But our first priority should be for the safety of Mrs Nuttall, then *after* that we go for the villains.

Carol   And that's what *you'd* do..? If you were in charge?[]

Dave   That's right, Ma'am. But for pity's sake don't say *I* said anything.

Carol   No, Sergeant. We won't… Now, hadn't you better ask me those questions?

Dave   I'd like to look around down here, first, Mrs Anderson. Perhaps you'd show me round.

Carol   Very well. This way. *(She leads off R.)*

Dave   *(as he follows her off R)* And try to remember not to touch anything.

(The lights dim stage R and come up stage L. Laura is sobbing by the door. The sound of the van returning is heard off L. Laura looks up and listens, then hastily gets to her feet. She runs to the "window" and looks out, but obviously cannot see anything. She goes back to the door and kicks on it.)

Laura   *(shouting)* Help me! Please! Help me! I'm in here!

(The bolts are drawn back. Laura stands back from the door. Barry enters L. As he enters, Laura makes a dash for the door, but Barry grabs her, one hand nearly covering her mouth.)

(shouting though the door, despite Barry's hand) Help me! Somebody! Help me!

Barry   You can scream the place down if you want. We're miles away from anywhere. Nobody'll hear you.

(Laura bites Barry's hand. He pulls it away in pain, then slaps her and flings her on the bed.)

(holding his hand) Bitch!

Laura   *(turning on the bed to face him)* Just untie my hands. I'll show you what a bitch I can be!

Barry   *(advancing on her; with sadistic glee)* I like them with a bit of fight. *(He takes hold of Laura's hair and twists her head to face him, making her scream out in pain. He rips her blouse away from her shoulder.)* I'll teach you to bite me. By the time I've finished with you, you'll be begging for mercy!

(Dianne enters L unseen by Barry or Laura and watches the scene. She is dressed in jeans and a man's shirt and has the pistol tucked in her belt. Barry is running his hands over Laura. He forces her face towards him and roughly kisses her, his hands all over her while she struggles to move away. When he has succeeded he lets her hair go. Laura spits in his face. Dianne is highly amused.)

Dianne   *(laughing)* I told you she'd spit in your face!

Barry   *(raising his hand as if to strike Laura)* I'll show the bitch!

(Laura cowers back.)

Dianne   Barry! No! Not now! Don't mark her! *(Barry keeps his hand up but does not strike her.)* We need a good photo of her so hubby'll play ball.

Barry   *(making as if to strike again)* A few nice bruises should convince him.

Dianne   *(restraining Barry's hand)* No! Not yet...! Next time, maybe, but not yet.

(Dianne lets Barry's hand go and turns away. Barry makes as if to strike again, making Laura cower once again, then withdraws his hand and turns away.)

Barry   *(whipping back to face Laura, pointing a warning finger at her)* I'll sort you out later. *(Sneering at her helplessness)* Maybe I'll have a sample of what a wife's like!

Dianne   *(to Barry)* Finished now?

Barry   *(to Dianne)* Stay out of it, Di. This is between me and her.

Dianne   Well sort it out some other time. For now we need her.

Laura   What d'you need me for? I've no money. You must have the wrong person.

Dianne *(sitting next to her on the bed)* Oh, no we haven't, my pretty. We've got the right one all right. We've been planning this one for months.

Laura But why? Please tell me.

Barry Don't tell her! Make the bitch squirm!

Dianne Piss off, Barry. You've already shown everyone you can beat up on a girl who can't defend herself. Just can it. Go and get the food.

Barry Let her starve!

Dianne I told you - we need her. *(With menace)* Now go and get the food!

(Barry casts a threatening glance at the women and reluctantly exits L.)

Don't mind him, love. He carries his brains around in his trousers.

Laura *(desperate)* What d'you want from me?

Dianne Nothing, love. Nothing. You're just our insurance policy, that's all.

Laura I don't know what you mean.

Dianne We've got you so your husband'll do *exactly* what we say.

Laura Roger? But he hasn't any money either.

Dianne Now that's where you're wrong. You keep saying you've got no money. That stupid frightened bitch back at your house kept on about it, too.

Laura *(remembering)* Carol…? You didn't hurt her? What did you do?

Dianne Nothing, love. She's O.K. Probably suffering a bit from cramp by now unless dear old Roger's home yet. But she's O.K.

Laura Oh, thank God.

Dianne *(amused at the memory)* Mind you, she nearly wet herself when I pointed this at her. *(She pats the pistol in her belt.)*

Laura You what!?

Dianne Don't worry, it's only… *(She stops herself)* The safety was on.

Laura What is it you want from Roger?

Dianne Times and dates. To start with, anyway.

Laura Times and dates of what?

Dianne My God, you *are* stupid, aren't you?

Laura *(reacting)* One of us must be. I don't know what you're on about.

Dianne *(pulling the gun from her belt; angry)* You want to watch your mouth, love. I said we need you, but we'll manage without you if we have to! *(She points the gun at Laura.)*

Laura *(trying to appease Dianne's anger)* All right! All right! I'm sorry… Please… put that away.

Dianne Scare you, does it, love?

Laura Y… yes.

Dianne *(infatuated with the gun's power over Laura)* Lovely things, these. Power in the palm of your hand. Nobody screws with you if you've got one of these. *(She weighs it in her hand, savouring the feel.)* Beautiful balance. Dead weight. *(Amused at her own joke)* "Dead weight"… get it..? But so cold. Cold.., hard.., *death*. You just feel how cold it is.

(Dianne strokes the gun barrel slowly across Laura's cheek. Laura recoils from the feel.)

Laura *(desperate)* Please, stop. Please. I'll do as you say. We both will.

Dianne *(tracing the gun down past Laura's neck, past the torn blouse until she has it between Laura's breasts)* Of course you will. See what I mean? Power.

Laura *(trying to lead the conversation away from the gun)* You… you were going to tell me what you want Roger to do.

Dianne *(continuing to stroke the gun over Laura's body)* You really can't guess, can you?

Laura No. I keep telling you!

Dianne What does hubby do for a living?

Laura Surely you already know that.

Dianne Tell me. Humour me.

Laura He's a manager at an electronics factory.

Dianne What sort of manager?

Laura Nothing important. He's in the Administration Department. He doesn't have anything to do with the electronics, so if you're trying to…

Dianne We're not interested in electronics.

Laura Then what?

Dianne What does your husband do on the last Thursday of every month?

Laura   *(puzzled)* I don't know. He goes to work same as every other day.

Dianne   Isn't the last Thursday of every month rather special to him? To both of you, in fact? Isn't it something to look forward to?

Laura   Well, of course it means it's payday, but apart from that... *(She realises; in horror)* Oh, God! You're going to steal the wages.

Dianne   First prize! Got it in one!

Laura   But you can't...! Anyway Roger doesn't handle the wages.

Dianne   We know that. But he does know the times and dates of the deliveries..., *and* the route that's taken. And he's got a key to the side gate.

Laura   But the Police... They'll be waiting for you.

Dianne   That's right, my pretty. That's what we *want* them to think. *(With sudden venom)* Stupid bastards!

Laura   I don't understand.

Dianne   *(normal again)* The Police think we just want him to unlock the gate. What he's *really* going to do is bring us the money when it arrives. Except we sort of.. haven't told him yet!

Laura   *(puzzled)* Why...?

Dianne   They'll think all they have to do is wait and we'll just turn up and walk into the nick. And in the meantime, while they're happy thinking that, they won't try too hard to find us, will they?

Laura   They'll follow him when he goes to meet you!

Dianne   Not if he ever wants to see you again they won't.

Laura   But he... Roger has never done anything wrong in his life! He wouldn't... He won't help you. I know he won't.

          (Dianne strokes the gun back up towards Laura's face. She holds the barrel to her lips. Laura recoils terrified.)

Dianne   I hope, for your sake, you don't know him as well as you think you do, 'cause if he doesn't help us... well, let's just say you won't be having any more birthday parties. *(She strokes the gun down Laura's neck to her chest.)* Barry fancies you, y'know... But don't worry, I won't let him near you... *if* you behave. *(She pulls the neckline of Laura's blouse apart and puts the barrel of the gun inside.)* Who knows...? I might even have you myself. I got quite a taste for pretty girls when I was in the nick.

Laura   Please...! Leave me alone!

(Dianne withdraws the gun from Laura's blouse and strokes the material back into position. It is an overtly sexual action. Laura shudders.)

Dianne For now. *(A pause.)* As long as hubby behaves.

Laura You're crazy! It'll never work.

Dianne Oh, yes it will, my love. It has before. This'll be the fifth time we've done this, and dear old hubby always delivers in the end.

Laura He won't! I know him!

Dianne That's what they all say at first. I remember the very first one. *He* didn't think we'd do it. "Robbery's one thing but murder's a life sentence," he said when we phoned him.

Laura That's true, you know. And if you'd let me go I'd never tell.

Dianne I convinced him I'd killed before.

Laura And had you?

Dianne I was *very* convincing. He did what we said in the end. But just to show him, he didn't get his wife back. Ever. So when anyone tries that crap on me now I can tell 'em… and I can be *really* convincing, can't I?

(Barry enters L with a plastic carrier bag with some containers from a takeaway food shop. He puts the bag on the table.)

(standing) About time too.

Barry I got her Chinese.

Dianne Did you get any forks?

Barry There's a plastic spoon in there. *(He indicates the carrier bag.)*

Dianne *(taking out the food and a spoon)* Good idea. We don't want Laura here hurting herself on metal ones, do we? *(to Laura)* What d'you fancy, love?

Laura I'm not hungry.

Barry *(a sneer)* Let her starve.

Dianne Look, love. You're going to be here a few days, so you might as well get used to it.

Laura *(determined)* I said I'm not hungry!

Dianne O.K. Suit yourself. Won't be our fault if you starve to death.

Laura Go to hell!

Dianne *(opening a container and trying the food; amused)* We probably will, my love. We probably will.

Barry *(eating)* But we'll have had a hell of a good time before we go, won't we, Di? *(He laughs inanely.)*

Dianne *(softening)* Look, love, you might as well have something to eat. *(She moves to Laura)* When we send you back to your husband you don't want to be ill, do you?

Barry *If* we send you back.

Dianne Can it, Barry. *(She holds a spoonful of rice towards Laura's mouth.)* Here, just have a try of this.

(Laura turns her head away to avoid the food.)

Barry *(standing)* Here, give that me. *(Taking the spoon)* I'll make her eat.

(Barry grabs Laura's hair and yanks her head back. He forces a spoonful of rice into her mouth. Laura coughs and splutters and spits the food out as she nearly chokes. Barry hurls her down on the bed where she coughs and sobs.)

Dianne You're a bloody animal at times, Barry.

Barry She deserves it… Silly cow!

Dianne Leave her alone for a bit, will you?

Barry I'm going down the pub for a pint. I'll make the call when I'm out.

Dianne Go, then. But don't come back pissed out of your brain. The last thing we want is you getting picked up as a drunk driver!

Barry No chance! The police round here are even more stupid than the London mob. They couldn't catch a cold! *(menacingly to Laura)* I'll see *you* later.

(Barry puts the food on the table and exits L. Laura is still sobbing. Dianne puts her food down and sits with her.)

Dianne Come on, love. Cheer up.

Laura Why the hell should you care?

Dianne Look, love. I know it's not pleasant for you, and I know you won't believe it but I'm sorry. It's just… well it's business, you see. We don't mean no harm.

Laura No harm!? Then why treat me like this?

Dianne I told you - it's business. Barry don't mean it either, really. He quite fancies you, you know. He told me. I think he was angry 'cause you wouldn't play ball.

Laura What the hell d'you expect!?

Dianne *(as if talking to a child)* I know love, I know. He'll calm down, just you see. Meantime, even though it's not pleasant, why not make the best of it, eh? You have some of this food. *(She picks up the container again.)*

Laura *(slightly less defiant)* I already told you…

Dianne I know you told me. But like I said… you've got to keep your strength up for when you see Roger again. *(She holds a fork of rice to Laura's mouth.)* Come on, try it.

(Laura, reluctantly at first, tries some of the food, then starts to slowly eat it.)

That's it, love. Nice, ain't it?

(Dianne continues to feed Laura as the action switches.)

(The doorbell rings off R.)

Maria *(off R; calling)* Sergeant! That's probably the phone recorder. See to it, will you?

Dave *(off R; calling)* Yes, Ma'am. On my way.

(The front door is heard to open off R, and a muffled conversation ensues. The door is heard to close and shortly afterwards Dave enters carrying the recorder, and earpiece, a box and wires, and a box of cassette tapes. Carol follows.)

Carol D'you know what to do?

Dave Yes, dead easy. I've done it loads of times. *(Over the next few lines, he reaches down, unplugs the telephone, plugs the recorder in and plugs the phone into the recorder box.)*

Carol Hadn't you better hurry? What happens if they phone while you're setting it up?

Dave *(glancing at his watch)* I've got a few minutes, yet.

Carol How d'you know?

Dave *(putting a tape in the machine)* I'll lay you odds they phone at seven. Strange thing about kidnappers - they always phone dead on the hour. As if it matters. So they'll phone in about two minutes or we'll have to wait another hour. Just you see.

(Maria and Roger enter R. Maria carries a framed photograph of Laura which she hands to Dave.)

Maria All linked up, Sergeant?

Dave Yes, Ma'am. All finished. The recorder comes on automatically when the phone rings. We can listen through this earpiece.

Roger Won't they know someone's listening?

Dave   No, sir. It's listen-only.

Carol   Sergeant Robinson reckons they'll ring dead on the hour.

Dave   They always do, Sir.

Roger   *(glancing at his watch)* But it's seven o'clock now.

(Right on cue, the telephone rings. Roger dashes towards it.)

Maria   One moment, sir. Try and keep them talking as long as possible. The exchange will try and trace the call.

Roger   Right. *(He goes to the telephone.)*

Maria   *(in a whisper)* Check it works, Sergeant.

(Dave watches the machinery, Maria puts the earpiece to her ear, and - on cue from Maria, Roger lifts the receiver.)

Roger   Hello… Yes, it is… What have you done with her…? Is she all right…? Let me speak to her… Please… I want to speak to my wife… Yes… Yes, I'll do anything you ask, only please don't hurt her… Yes… No…! No… don't go…! Hello! Hello! *(He lowers the receiver.)* They hung up.

Maria   *(to Dave)* Go and call in. See if they got a trace.

Dave   No chance! They were too quick.

Maria   *(insistent)* Go and see!

(Dave exits R.)

Carol   What did they say? Is she all right?

Roger   They *say* she is. They're going to ring back in the morning. *(to Maria; appealing)* Why wouldn't they tell me what they wanted? I said I'd co-operate.

Maria   That's not unusual. They want to make you uneasy.

Roger   They succeeded.

Maria   *(removing the tape from the recorder and replacing it with a new one)* We'll take this down to the lab., see if they can get anything.

Roger   *Were* they on long enough to trace the call?

Maria   I doubt it. But we may be able to get the general area.

Carol   *(taking Roger's hand)* Don't worry, Roger. She'll be O.K.

(Dave enters R carrying his open notebook.)

Maria   Well?

Dave   We didn't get the full number…

Roger Damn!

Dave No, wait a minute. We may be in luck. The call was from a fairly deserted area, and from a public callbox. There aren't that many callboxes in that area.

Roger Does that help?

Maria It might. Each time they call we can get a more accurate fix.

Dave *If* they use the same call box.

Roger Is that likely?

Maria To be honest, probably not. But even so we'll know the area to look. If we can get a trace we can start a search.

Roger It was very noisy, wherever it was.

Maria Yes, I noticed that. I may be wrong, but I'm sure I heard glasses in the background. They could have used a pub phone.

Dave Or a café.

Carol There, you see, Roger... They're getting closer already.

Roger I hope to God they won't be too late.

Maria I don't think there's any more we can do until morning, sir, so I think we'll go and let our experts have a listen to the tape. I doubt if they'll call again before tomorrow, but if they should, the machine will do the rest and the exchange will do the trace.

Roger Right. I'll try to keep them on again.

Maria *(taking a card from her pocket)* Give us a call if anything happens. Here's my direct number.

Roger *(taking the card)* O.K. Thanks.

Maria I really don't think you should be on your own tonight, Mr Nuttall. Is there anyone you could call?

Carol I'll stay with him.

Roger No, please... I'd rather be alone.

Maria Very well, sir, as you please. We'll see you in the morning. *(She places a reassuring hand on his arm.)* Don't give up hope... we'll get her back.

Dave Good night, Sir... Ma'am.

Roger Good night.

(Maria and Dave exit R. The front door is heard to open and close, then a car starts and draws away.)

Carol Are you sure you'll be O.K?

Roger   Yes. I've got some thinking to do.

Carol   Why don't you come and stay with us?

Roger   No, I can't… They might ring.

Carol   D'you want me to stay?

Roger   No. I'll be all right. *(He wanders over to the "window".)*

Carol   You're sure?

Roger   *(looking out and upwards)* The moon's up.

Carol   *(puzzled)* What?

Roger   The moon. Whenever Laura and I have been apart, like when I've been working away, we always used to agree to look at the moon. It was… sort of… like looking at each other. We were in different places, but it was the same moon.

(Carol is overcome and goes to Roger. She puts her arms around him and sobs into his shoulder.)

Carol   She *will* be all right, Roger.

Roger   God, I hope so, Carol. I hope so. *(He stands Carol upright and offers her his handkerchief.)* Come on, you'd better be getting back home. *(Slightly bitter)* I don't want to break your marriage up as well.

Carol   *(drying her eyes)* Yes, all right. I'll come round in the morning. 'Bye, Roger. *(She kisses him on the cheek.)*

Roger   'Bye, Carol.

Carol   *(going towards the door R)* Call us if anything happens.

Roger   *(following her off R; as they exit)* I will… Pray for us.

(The food tray is empty and Dianne screws it up and throws it in a corner.)

Dianne That's a good girl. Feeling better now?

Laura   Yes… Thanks…

Dianne Now, I'm going up to join Barry down the pub.

Laura   *(afraid)* No! Don't leave me!

Dianne You'll be all right, love. Nobody can get in here… *(With a laugh)* Or out!

Laura   *(pleading again)* Please let me go.

Dianne Now we've already gone through all that. We'll let you go when we've got the money. Now you settle down and get some rest. *(She stands and goes to the door L.)* I'll check on you when we get back. *(She opens the door and, as she exits)* Or Barry will… Don't go away now.

(Dianne exits L, laughing, and closes the door behind her. The heavy bolts are heard to close and her footsteps recede. All is silent. Roger enters R, sad and low and sits in the armchair. Laura rises from the bed and listens at the door. She turns her back to it and tries unsuccessfully to open it. She goes to the centre of the room.)

Roger *(close to despair)* Oh, Laura, Laura… Where are you? What have they done to you?

Laura Roger… please do what they say.

(Laura wanders over to the "window". She looks up and sees the moon rise.)

(Tearful) Oh, Roger…!

(They both stand facing each other, staring out of their respective "windows" at the moon, remembering the past.)

Roger *(to the moon; calling plaintively)* Laura… where are you?

The curtain falls

ACT II

The following morning. The set is as ACT I. The lights are up stage L and down stage R. As the curtain rises, Laura is asleep on the bed. The bolts on the door L are heard to draw back and Dianne and Barry enter. Barry carries an instant camera and a small tape recorder. Dianne carries a slip of paper and a cup of coffee.

Dianne *(stern)* Wake her up.

Barry *(with childish glee)* Yeah. Wake her up! *(Puts the recorder and camera on the table and goes to Laura. He roughly shakes her until she stirs.)*

Dianne Morning, my love. And how are we this lovely morning?

Laura Tired, cold and uncomfortable.

Dianne You should have said. I'm sure Barry would have come and warmed you up. Eh, Barry?

Barry *(interested)* Yeah!

Dianne *(laughing)* Or *I* would!

Laura   My hands have gone dead. Can't you untie me? I can't exactly go anywhere, can I?

Dianne Sorry, my love. We don't want you hurting yourself falling out of a window, do we?

Barry   Or running out the door as soon as we open it.

Laura   Just for a minute, then. Get my circulation back.

Dianne *(suddenly annoyed)* I said "No!"

Barry   *(to Laura)* Don't you upset Di… Di's not very nice when she gets upset, are you Di?

Dianne Piss off, Barry.

Barry   See what I mean?

Dianne Now, we just want to take a couple of photographs of you. So Roger can see we haven't hurt you. Get the camera, Barry.

Barry   Right. The camera.

Dianne *(going to Laura and pulling her into a sitting position)* Now, you sit up and give Roger a nice big smile. Ready, Barry?

Barry   *(focusing the camera)* I'm ready. *(He cannot get a clear shot.)* You'll have to move, Di… I can see you an' all.

Laura   *(as Dianne leaves her)* I'll be damned if I'll help you! *(She falls over back onto the bed so her face cannot be seen.)*

Barry   Hold the stupid bitch still!

Dianne *(going to Laura and shaking her upright; angry)* Keep still! *(Laura still will not pose. With barely controlled rage)* Look, love, I don't give a toss whether he gets a photo of you like this, or with a few bruises here and there. *(Giving vent to her anger)* Now sit up and sit still!

            (Dianne sits Laura upright and gives her a stinging slap. Laura falls sideways from the blow, and sobs into the bed. Dianne raises her hand again to attack.)

            Sit up, you bitch!

Laura   *(cringing)* No! Don't!

Dianne Then bloody-well sit up!

Barry   *(lowering the camera; a first glimmer of compassion)* Di! That's enough!

Dianne Sod off Barry! Stay out of it!

            (Dianne raises her hand to strike again, but Barry grabs hold of it He is very strong.)

Barry   Enough, Di. She'll sit up, now. Won't you, love?

(Laura manages to nod her head between sobs.)

Dianne *(trying to get at her)* I'll show the cow!

Barry   *(struggling with Dianne; attempting to calm her)* Di, we need the photos. Here, you take the camera. *(He gives her the camera.)* And I'll lift her up.

Dianne *(reluctantly taking the camera; still enraged)* All right! *You* do it! But I swear, if she does that again I'll send her back in little pieces.

Barry   She won't do it again, will you?

Laura   *(surprised at his attitude)* No. No, I promise.

(Dianne calms herself and moves L to take the photo.)

Barry   *(helping Laura to a sitting position)* Come on now. We've had enough trouble for today. You just do what we say and it'll soon be over.

Laura   *(sobbing)* Please let me go.

Dianne *(aiming the camera)* Get out of the way, Barry!

Barry   *(to Laura; soothing)* You sit up and have your photo took.

(Barry moves L, leaving Laura in a sitting position. Dianne prepares to shoot. Laura's head is bowed.)

Dianne *(still shouting)* Put your head up! Towards the camera! Barry, sort the cow out, or *I* will!

Laura   *(jerking her head up in fear)* All right! All right!

Dianne That's better. *(She takes a photo.)*

Barry   What about the tape?

Dianne In a minute! Let's check this has come out first.

(Barry reaches towards the photo as it comes from the camera.)

(Stopping him) The edges! Just hold it by the edges! We don't want your paw-prints all over it.

(They watch as the print develops.)

Barry   That looks O.K.

Dianne I'll take one more. Just in case. *(Dianne takes another shot while Laura sits subdued and broken.)* Right. I'm going to do the letter. You sort the tape out. I've written it down on here. *(She gives Barry the slip of paper.)* Make sure that's *all* she says.

Barry   She can't tell nobody where she is, can she? She was out cold for the whole journey.

Dianne Just make sure that's *all* she says. She knows our names and what we look like, remember.

Barry I'll make sure.

Dianne And make sure you don't get your voice on it. The police may be stupid, but their lab. people aren't!

Barry Di..! Stop worrying! I'll sort it. Now go!

Dianne *(to Laura; suddenly full of venom again)* And *you*... behave!

Barry *(easing her out of the door L)* Di! Go!

(Dianne exits L. Barry picks up the recorder. After a pause he pulls the chair across and sits opposite Laura.)

You all right, love?

Laura *(she nods and sniffs.)* Why did she hit me?

Barry Di gets a bit worked up now and again. She don't mean it.

Laura She wasn't like that last night.

Barry No, I told you... She gets worked up. You do as you're told and... and you'll be O.K.

Laura D'you mean that?

Barry Yes, course I do.

Laura You're not going to let me go, are you?

Barry Course we are. As soon as your husband does his bit we'll phone him and tell him where to find you.

Laura I don't believe you.

Barry Look.., we don't want to hurt no-one. It's one thing risking getting put away for this sort of job, but *(hesitates)* murder's something else. No way I'm going to risk life.

Laura But your friend... she said that she'd already... *(She cannot bring herself to say "killed".)*

Barry Don't take no notice of her. She just did it to scare you. She likes scaring people, does Di.

Laura Why d'you stay with her?

Barry Why not?

Laura You're not like her.

Barry She's O.K. *(obviously repeating what Dianne has told him many times)* She looks after me. She's good for me.

Laura   She's no good for anyone.

Barry   Don't you let her hear you talk like that. No sense in making her angry. *(He takes the recorder and the paper.)* Now, we got to get this tape done.

Laura   What is it?

Barry   You're going to send a message to your husband. Di's written down what you've got to say on here. *(He shows her the paper.)* You just make sure you can read it first. *(Barry holds up the paper and Laura reads it.)* O.K?

Laura   Yes. Can't I just tell him…?

Barry   You tell him *exactly* what it says on the paper. No more, no less. And if I were you I shouldn't sound too upset. We don't want him doing nothing silly, do we now?

Laura   All right. I'll do as you say.

Barry   Good girl. *(He gets the recorder ready.)* Right, when I press this button you just talk into it. *(He switches on the recorder and holds it towards Laura. He holds up the paper and indicates for her to start.)*

Laura   *(reading; fairly controlled)* Roger… This is Laura… I'm all right and they're treating me well… You'll get another phone call after you get this tape, telling you what you've got to do. If you do it they'll tell you where to find me. If you don't they're going to kill me. Please do as they say, Roger. *(She has finished reading, but, in a rush, adds)* Look at the moon, my darling. I love you.

(Barry quickly whips the recorder away and turns it off. He checks what was written.)

Barry   *(annoyed)* I thought I said to just read the paper! We'll have to do it again, now. *(He rewinds the tape.)*

Laura   Please leave it on.

Barry   No. *(Suspicious)* It's some sort of clue you're giving him, ain't it?

Laura   No, no it's not. What could I possibly tell him? I don't *know* anything. Please leave it.

Barry   What's it mean, then?

Laura   Whenever we've been apart we always agreed we'd look at the moon at night. That way we'd know we were both looking at the same thing.

Barry   That's stupid.

Laura   To you, maybe. But it helped us. And it'll help Roger now… *And* me… Please leave it.

Barry Di'll go crackers.

Laura Don't tell her! Why does she have to know? *(Barry is weakening. Pleading)* Please…

Barry All right, then. Can't do no harm, I s'pose.

Laura Thank you… *(a first attempt to win him over)* Barry.

Barry *(standing)* Now, you stay here and I'll go and pack this up. *(He lifts Laura's feet back on the bed.)*

Laura Can't you untie me?

Barry No! You heard what Di said.

Laura Just for a few minutes… get my circulation going? She'd never know.

Barry *(finally; his violent attitude back again)* No! *(He exits L and the bolts are heard to close L.)*

(Laura sinks back into the bed. The lights dim stage L and come up stage R. The front door bell rings off R. Footsteps are heard running down the stairs off R and the front door is heard to open off R.)

Roger *(off R; weary)* Oh, Carol…

Carol *(off R)* Any news?

Roger No, nothing… Come in.

(The front door is heard to close and Carol enters R. Roger follows her in. He is dressed in the same clothes as in Act I, but looks as though he has slept in them.)

Carol You look awful. Have you slept?

Roger Have you?

Carol Not really. Let me make us some coffee.

(Carol exits R. Roger paces the room, his mind elsewhere. Distant kitchen sounds can be heard off R over the next few lines.)

(off R) Why don't you go up and freshen up?

Roger What for?

Carol It'll make you feel better.

Roger I don't feel like it. I don't want to feel better.

Carol You can't just give up, Roger. Life must go on.

Roger   *(looking heavenwards)* Oh, please let that be so.

Carol   If... *(she corrects herself)* When Laura comes back you'll have to be strong for her.

Roger   I will be. I'll never let her out of my sight again.

Carol   *(entering R carrying a tray of cups, etc.)* It's bound to have been traumatic for her.

Roger   Let's just get her back first. It'll be all right if she comes back.

Carol   I've put the kettle on. Some coffee'll help.

Roger   *(with a glance at his watch)* Where's that damned woman?

Carol   The policewoman?

Roger   Yes. I thought she'd have been here by now. What the hell's keeping her?

Carol   *(after a pause; tentatively)* What d'you think of her?

Roger   Not much. She was much too matter-of-fact for my liking.

Carol   They probably see this sort of thing all the time. They probably get hardened to it.

Roger   If they see it all the time you'd think they'd be able to do something, wouldn't you?

Carol   That Sergeant... *(She stops.)*

Roger   What about him?

Carol   Oh, nothing.

Roger   *(forceful; not to be argued with)* What about him?

Carol   He said he... He doesn't think she can handle it.

Roger   What!?

Carol   He said she's got no experience. He reckons she's more interested in arresting the kidnappers than getting Laura back safely.

Roger   *(near breaking point)* Oh, my God, that's all we need.

Carol   What can we do?

Roger   I'll tackle her about it, that's what.

Carol   The Sergeant said not to say anything.

Roger   *(furious)* I don't give a damn what he said. We've got Laura to think of.

Carol   *(going to him, her hand on his shoulder)* All right, Roger, calm down. We'll sort it out between us... We will.

Roger   *(responding)* I'm sorry, Carol, I don't mean to get at you, but, don't you see..? I'm going crazy without her.

Carol   *(sits him in chair)* We'll get her back, Roger... We *have* to.

Roger   Please God.

Carol   Now you sit there and I'll make that coffee. *(Exits R.)*

Roger   *(immediately stands and moves about the room. He examines the phone recorder.)* I hope this thing still works.

Carol   *(off R; not hearing)* What..? Wait a second... *(She enters R carrying a coffee pot.)* Now, what did you say?

Roger   I said I hope this thing's still working. What if they try and phone and it's broken?

Carol   Roger, it works! You've got to put your trust in something. You'll drive yourself mad if you go on like this.

         (Carol pours two cups of coffee. There is the noise of letters being posted through the letter-box off R.)

Roger   *(with a start)* What was that?

Carol   It was only the postman. My God, you're jumpy. Here... drink this. *(She hands him his coffee.)*

Roger   I'm not thirsty.

Carol   Drink it!

Roger   *(takes the coffee and wanders over to the "window" C.)* I hope they're feeding her.

Carol   They will do. They've got to keep her alive until we've met their demands...

Roger   Whatever they are!

Carol   So she must be safe until then. Whatever you do you must insist on speaking to her. They can't refuse that.

Roger   If they've hurt her I'll... I'll...

Carol   *(reassuring)* She'll be O.K., Roger. She's strong.

         (The doorbell rings off R.)

Roger   Now what?

Carol   It's probably the police. I'll let them in. *(She moves R.)*

Roger   Try and get rid of the Sergeant. I'll tackle the woman.

Carol   All right. *(Exits R. After a moment Carol enters R carrying a small package and two letters. Maria follows, carrying a black document case.)*

It's the Inspector, Roger. The Sergeant isn't here.

Maria Good morning, Mr Nuttall.

Roger *(frosty)* Morning, Inspector.

Carol Here's the post, Roger. *(Hands the post to him. He distractedly puts them down on top of the television.)*

Maria Any more calls, sir?

Roger No, nothing.

Maria Good, then I'm not too late.

Roger *(still frosty)* Yes, we don't want you to risk missing out on your arrests, do we?

Maria *(puzzled)* Er.., no, sir.

Roger Have you, er… any *experience* of this sort of case, Inspector?

Maria I've had full training in all aspects of…

Carol That *wasn't* what he asked!

Roger I said *experience*, Inspector, not training.

Maria I can assure you, Mr Nuttall that the training we're given in all types of crime is of the highest order and based on real cases…

Roger *(interrupting)* I'm not interested in your assurances, Inspector. I want my wife back.

Maria So do I, sir. And that's what we'll get.

Carol *And* a few arrests to go with it!

Maria Hopefully we shall, Ma'am.

Roger *(steeling himself)* You're not interested in Laura's safety at all, are you!? You're cold and dispassionate.

Maria *(outraged)* I can assure you, Mr Nuttall…

Roger *(interrupting)* I told you… I don't want your assurances.

Maria Nevertheless, you'll get them… I realise you're in an emotional condition…

Roger Generous of you!

Maria But I'll tell you now, it is my intention to get your wife back, as soon and as safe as possible.

Carol And what about your arrest record?

Maria We shall, of course, try our utmost to apprehend the culprits.

Roger I don't give a damn about them. It's Laura that matters.

Maria   An understandable sentiment, Mr Nuttall, but I have to consider the whole picture.

Carol   Meaning Laura's a side issue!?

Maria   What *is* the matter with you? I've told you, first and most important we get Laura back. Second, but still important, we get these people and put them away. Maybe you don't care what happens to them, but I have to.

Roger   They can rot in hell for all I care.

Maria   Let's say all goes well and we get Laura back safe and well... But the villains get away.

Roger   Suits me.

(Carol nods her agreement.)

Maria   Yes, of course it suits *you*! But imagine what could happen. You're all living happily ever after and all of a sudden there's some other poor sod out there whose wife gets taken. And then another. And then some other lot gets to hear of it and think they'll have a go. Before you know it we've got a new national pastime.

Roger   *(softening)* I know you think I'm selfish, but..

Maria   Of course you're selfish. Who wouldn't be in your position? You've got a part to play in the events of the next few days... a very important part. Your wife's life may depend on what you do.

Roger   Don't you think I know that?

Maria   But *I've* got a rôle to play as well. It may not be as important as yours, but your wife's life still depends on it. You called me cold and dispassionate just now. I hope I'm not, but as far as your wife's safety goes, *you* can't be expected to be totally rational.

Roger   What d'you expect..?

Maria   I don't *expect* anything. You're holding up very well. But someone *does* have to be rational.

Carol   And that's where you come in?

Maria   Yes, Mrs Anderson, that's where I come in.

(Carol is unconvinced and goes idly to the television and looks at the post. Roger has calmed down and is sorry.)

Roger   I'm sorry, Inspector, I'm not thinking straight.

Maria   That's all right, sir. I understand.

Roger   And you're *sure* you're doing everything you can?

Maria   By the book, sir. The police procedures on these matters were written by much better minds than mine and based on actual case histories. The procedures are quite clear - our first priority should be for the safety of Mrs Nuttall, then *after* that we go for the culprits.

Carol   *(surprised)* But Sergeant Robinson said… *(She stops.)*

Maria   *(realising) What* did Sergeant Robinson say?

Carol   He said it was the other way round. Arrests first, safety last.

Maria   So *that's* where all this has come from. Good old Sergeant Robinson. What did he tell you?

Carol   I promised I wouldn't say anything.

Maria   You don't have to. I'll tell *you* what he said. It would be something along the lines of I've not been on the force long enough, straight out of college, no experience… Need I go on?

Carol   No. You've made your point. But why would he say all that?

Maria   I'm afraid there's still a lot of prejudice against women in the force, Mrs Anderson.

Roger   Why d'you have to fight your bloody battles at our expense!?

Maria   I'm sorry, sir. I wish I could have prevented this, but I can't. All I can do is apologise and assure you that Sergeant Robinson will be made to account for his behaviour.

Carol   Fat lot of good that will do us!

Roger   Inspector…

Maria   Sir?

Roger   Can I ask you a frank question?

Maria   If you wish, sir.

Roger   Can you get her back? Are you the best… *(He pauses.)*

Maria   The best *man* for the job, Mr Nuttall?

Roger   You know what I mean.

Maria   I don't know if I am, sir. I know I've had the training, and despite what has been said I do have plenty of police experience. All I can tell you is that I shall do my best to get her back. Cold and dispassionate I may appear, but seeing people like you in situations like this eats me up. But… if you decide you want someone else, a man if you like, then I'll ask to be replaced. It's only a matter of a telephone call.

Roger   *(after a pause exchanging glances with Carol)* No. I'd like you to stay. *(Another pause.)* And I'm sorry.

Carol   Me too.

Maria   There's really no need. Now, to business, if we may. *(Sits on the settee and takes a multi-page typed document from her case. Roger sits next to her.)*

Now, we've had the tape of the phone call analysed. Our suspicions were correct - it was a pub. And we may have had a stroke of luck.

Roger   About time something went right. What?

Maria   Our people managed to filter out the main voice and concentrate on the background noise. Someone says what sounds very much like "Appleby's".

Roger   What does that mean?

Maria   It's a type of beer.

Roger   Never heard of it.

Maria   No, nor had we. Apparently it's one of these strong ales, and it's sold at very few places. In the area we already got from the phone trace we've narrowed it down to four possible pubs.

Roger   *(impressed)* That's incredible!

Maria   We've sent men out to make discreet enquiries.

(Carol notices the package. She picks it up and looks at it.)

Roger   How important is this? It still doesn't tell us where she is.

Maria   No, true, but it narrows it down considerably. When they call again we should get more clues. The more we get, the closer we get.

Carol   *(holding the package)* Roger...

Roger   *(snapping; still more interested in Maria)* Yes?

Carol   Have you seen this?

Roger   What?

Carol   This package in the post.

Roger   I haven't got time for that now.

Carol   But it came with two letters, and...

Roger   *(irritated)* Carol! Does it matter now?

Carol   But look! The package has no stamp, or postmark.

Roger   So?

Carol   So it can't have come with the post.

Roger   *(standing)* Let me see that! *(He holds out his hand.)*

(Carol is just about to give him the package.)

Maria   Wait! *(They stop.)* Let me open it. There may be prints. *(to Carol)* Don't touch the package anywhere else! Just hold it. *(She gets a pair of polythene gloves and a few plastic bags from her case. She lays one of the bags on the table. She takes the package from Carol and puts it on one of the bags, then she opens the package, takes out the tape and checks the packet. A typewritten note falls out. She puts the packing in a second bag and seals it.)* Have you got a machine to play this?

Roger   Yes. *(He gets a radio cassette player from the shelf.)* Will this do?

Maria   Yes. That's fine.

(Maria puts the tape carefully in the machine and switches it on. Laura'S speech is heard. "Roger… This is Laura… I'm all right and they're treating me well… You'll get another phone call after you get this tape, telling you what you've got to do. If you do it they'll tell you where to find me. If you don't they're going to kill me. Please do as they say, Roger. Look at the moon, my darling. I love you." The tape goes silent.)

Carol   What does the letter say?

Maria   *(carefully picks up the note and unfolds it. Reading)* "So there you are, Roger, my love. We've got your precious wife. As she told you, she's all right - for the moment, and she'll stay all right as long as you do exactly as we say. I've no doubt you've got some stupid policeman sitting there with you - well you can tell them not to bother. They'll never find us - the tape and the note's got no fingerprints on them, and we're so well hidden we could stay here for months. Now, I suppose you're wondering what we want. Simple. We want money - the wages from your works to be exact. We'll phone with the details. Don't forget - no co-operation, no Laura." That's it.

Roger   The wages! I can't do that!

Carol   Roger! You've got to!

Maria   It would be best for your wife if you co-operate, Mr Nuttall. For the moment at least.

Roger   *(frantic)* But I don't deal with the wages! Not directly, anyway.

Maria   These people don't seem the type to make that sort of mistake.

They must think you can help them in some way.

Carol   Perhaps they've got someone else's wife as well - someone who works with you.

Maria   That's a possibility. I'll check whether anyone else has gone absent.

(The telephone rings.)

Carol   That might be them!

(Roger dashes to the phone and lifts the receiver. Maria listens on the earpiece.)

Maria   Don't forget, now. Keep them talking.

Roger   *(into the receiver)* Yes...? Yes it is. Now look here... Yes I have... Yes, we've just listened to it. Now look here you bastard, if you hurt Laura I'll... hello... *(Desperate)* Hello. *(Hopelessly to Maria and Carol)* They hung up. *(He replaces the receiver.)* Oh, my God!

Maria   *(replacing the earpiece)* They'll ring back.

Roger   What if they don't?

Maria   They will. Trust me. But you must curb your temper. Getting mad won't help anyone. When they ring, apologise.

Carol   *(incredulous)* What!?

Maria   *(firmly)* You must. Don't make them angry, whatever you do. They'll only take it out on Laura.

(The telephone rings again. Roger grabs the receiver. Maria picks up the earpiece.)

Roger   Hello, yes... Yes, it is... *(with difficulty)* Yes, I know... and I'm sorry. I'm just upset because of Laura... No, no I won't. Just don't hurt her... Please... Yes, but look, I can't... But don't you see, I don't have a key... Yes... yes all right, I will... Thursday, yes... Can I speak to Laura...? Please, I've got to speak to her...? How do I know if she's still.. if she's all right..? *(Breaking down)* Please *(He trails off.)*

(Roger breaks down and sobs, letting the receiver hang loosely in his hand. Maria replaces her earpiece and takes the receiver from Roger. She taps the rest and dials quickly on the phone. Carol takes a sobbing Roger to the settee and sits him down. She comforts him.)

Maria   *(into the receiver)* Inspector Pearson. Any luck...? No... no... Look, he couldn't. We're not dealing with amateurs here...

Yes... Oh, well that's a help I suppose... Yes, thanks. No, they didn't give a time. Right. 'Bye. *(She replaces the receiver.)*

Carol   Anything?

Maria   Not much, I'm afraid. They confirm it's the same area, but it wasn't the same number. *(She stands.)* Let's get these tapes to the Lab.

Carol   What can we do?

Maria   Nothing. Just wait for their call. *(After a thoughtful pause)* It's just... *(She trails off.)*

Carol   Just what..?

Maria   Well, they seem to know we'll be listening, and they must know how easy it would be for us to trap them.

Carol   So...?

Maria   I don't like it. They're making it too easy.

Carol   But they've got Laura, so they must know...

Roger   Don't let them hurt her! You won't do anything...!

Maria   *(still pensive)* No, no, of course not. We'll just have to wait and see what they say. *(She puts the tape in the polythene bag and puts the bags in her case, then takes the tape from the phone recorder and puts in a new one. She puts that tape in her case as well and closes it.)* I'll be back as soon as I can. With any luck we'll get some more from all this. I suggest you get some sleep, Mr Nuttall. I know it's difficult, but you need to be alert.

Carol   Don't worry. I'll get him to bed.

Maria   *(making for the door R)* Good. Don't leave him alone if you can help it. See you later, Mr Nuttall.

(Roger is still sobbing and does not reply.)

If anything else happens, give me a call.

Carol   I will.

Roger   Wait!

Maria   *(comes back to him.)* What? What is it?

Roger   It's hopeless. I *can't* do what they say.

Carol   Why? What do they want?

Roger   They want me to open the side gate and a door at work, then wait in the Wages Office for them.

Carol   So...? I don't see...

Roger   *(frantic)* Don't you understand? I *can't* unlock the gate - I don't have the key!

Maria   Don't worry, Mr Nuttall, we'll sort all that out.

Roger   You!? What can you do!?

Maria   Your wife must come first. I shall talk to your bosses, get them to co-operate.

Roger   You must be joking. No way that money-grabbing lot are going to risk losing their wages.

Maria   I'm quite sure I can persuade them.

Roger   I wish you luck.

Maria   I'll call them from the station. I'll see you later.

(Maria exits R. The front door opens and closes off R. Carol looks sympathetically at Roger then sits next to him.)

Carol   Come on, Roger. We're getting there.

Roger   *(a broken man)* Are we?

Carol   You must get some sleep.

Roger   Sleep!? How can I sleep?

Carol   You must.

Roger   D'you imagine Laura's slept?

Carol   *(coaxing)* Stop it, Roger. This won't help her. Now, I'll stay down here - you go on up to bed for an hour. *(She attempts to get him to stand.)*

Roger   No!

Carol   Roger, please…

Roger   No! I am *not* going away from that phone.

Carol   But I'll be here. I could call you.

Roger   *No!*

Carol   *(with a sigh)* All right. But at least lie back and try to sleep.

(Roger allows Carol to lie him back on the settee, where he stares into space.)

I'll go and make some tea. Calm your nerves.

(Roger does not reply, so Carol exits R. Over the next dialogue in the other room, Roger drifts off to an uneasy sleep. The lights dim stage R and come up stage L. Laura sits up on the bed. The bolts can be heard drawing back on the door L. Laura swings

her legs to the floor. The door L opens and Barry enters. He carries a mug of tea.)

Laura   Have you sent it?

Barry   Yeah. Di took it a bit ago.

Laura   Did she...? *(trails off)*

Barry   Don't worry... she didn't listen to it. *(pause)* I brought you some tea.

Laura   Thanks.

Barry   *(feeds the tea to Laura. There are several moments of silence.)* She's an odd woman.

Laura   Who? Di?

Barry   Yes. One minute she's nice as pie, then the next... I dunno.

Laura   Are you and she... well, you know?

Barry   Yeah... Well, we used to be, but these days... who knows?

Laura   Are you married?

Barry   Me? No. Never had the need.

Laura   You should. Everyone should.

Barry   Like you two, you mean?

Laura   And why not? What's wrong with Roger and me?

Barry   Poky little house in a poky little road. No money. Poxy car. No thanks. I want more than that.

(Laura has finished her tea. Barry takes the mug and puts it on the table.)

Laura   You should try it.

Barry   No thanks.

Laura   Have you ever been in love?

Barry   I dunno 'bout that... Love's for kids.

Laura   Haven't you ever been absolutely devoted to someone...? Have you ever had a woman devoted to *you*?

Barry   *(almost embarrassed)* No..! 's silly!

Laura   *(standing and going towards him)* Never..? Don't you think you've missed something?

Barry   No. Not really.

Laura   Imagine a woman who would do anything for you - satisfy your every desire. Imagine that.

Barry   Is that what you do for 'im… for Roger?

Laura   *(close to him)* I'd do it for *you* if you'd let me go.

Barry   *(moving away)* Now don't start none of that. You heard what Di said.

Laura   *(following)* Di, Di, Di! Haven't you got a mind of your own?

Barry   'Course I have.

Laura   Are you scared of her?

Barry   Me? No, course not.

Laura   Then why not take me?

Barry   *(pushing her away)* Because I don't want to.

Laura   You wanted to last night.

Barry   That were different.

Laura   Of course it was different. Last night I'd have fought you every bit of the way.

Barry   But not today?

Laura   That's right. You can have me. Anything you want. Anything at all. Only one condition.

Barry   What's that?

Laura   That afterwards you let me go.

Barry   You'd do that for *me?*

Laura   Yes. I won't fight.

Barry   No, I can't let you go.

Laura   Why not?

Barry   She'd kill me.

Laura   I said you were scared of her.

Barry   *(enraged)* I *ain't* scared of her.

(Barry suddenly grabs Laura and kisses her fiercely on the lips, running his hands over her body. He kisses her neck and shoulders, while Laura tries to feign enthusiasm. The embrace becomes more tender until eventually Laura is the one who is maintaining it. Eventually Barry stops and pulls away. Unknown to Laura - yet - he is afraid she will turn out like his mother, so it is "his mother" he pushes away. Laura tries to follow.)

Laura   What's wrong?

Barry   *(sullen)* I can't do it.

Laura   You can... You want me. You can't hide it.

Barry   Yeah, I do, but...

Laura   But what...? But Di might find out?

Barry   It ain't Di... It's you.

Laura   Me...? What's wrong with me?

Barry   *(sitting on the bed; embarrassed)* I... I sort of... *respect* you.

Laura   *(incredulous)* You *respect* me!? You drag me here unconscious..., you slap me about and virtually try to rape me..., you're using me to get Roger to help you do a robbery, and... you *respect* me!?

Barry   Yeah.

Laura   So now you don't want me?

Barry   *(standing and moving away from her)* It ain't that...

Laura   Then take me! I'm asking you!

(Laura goes to Barry, stands in front of him and does her best to rub herself against him and kiss him. He pushes her away.)

Barry   *(determined)* No!

Laura   I give up!

Barry   I don't want to take another man's woman.

Laura   It didn't seem to bother you last night!

Barry   *(sitting on the bed)* That were different.

Laura   Why, for God's sake?

Barry   I didn't know you then.

Laura   You didn't...? *(She shakes her head.)* But you know me now?

Barry   Yeah.

Laura   And that makes a difference?

Barry   Yeah, I told you, I respect you. I don't want to hurt you... I thought you were like *her*.

Laura   *(puzzled)* Her?

Barry   *(insistent)* Yeah... *Her!*

Laura   Who...? Dianne?

Barry   *(impatient)* No, not Dianne... *Her*...! My mum!

Laura   *(baffled)* Your mum? I'm like your mother?

Barry   *(quickly)* No! Not like her. *(pause)* I just *thought* you were... last night.

Laura　But I'm not?

Barry　*(hurting)* No.

Laura　Didn't you like your mother?

Barry　No… She were cheap.

Laura　Cheap?

Barry　She had men. Hundreds of 'em… She hated me.

Laura　I'm sure she didn't…

Barry　*(quickly; insistent)* She *hated* me!

Laura　What about your father?

Barry　Never had one.

Laura　He left you?

Barry　I dunno. She never talked about him. If I asked she used to hit me.

Laura　Why?

Barry　I dunno. Never found out.

(They both pause, Laura lost for words and Barry deep in painful thoughts.)

No father… just lots of uncles… *(pause)* She *hated* me… I got in her way, see..? She made me watch.

Laura　*(puzzled)* Watch?

Barry　We only had one room. I had to watch her with her men. They used to laugh at me… *(pause)* She were cheap.

Laura　Did you run away?

Barry　They threw me out. Her and this bloke decided to live together, and there weren't no room for me. Only one room, y'see? So I had to go.

Laura　What did you do?

Barry　Dunno… Can't remember.

Laura　Did you ever see her again?

Barry　*(quietly)* When she were dead.

Laura　She died?

Barry　She were beaten up. Some bloke I s'pose. She died… *(Brighter)* I saw her when she were dead.

Laura   *(genuinely shocked)* That's awful.

Barry   *(bitter)* I'm *glad* she died. She deserved it. *(pause)*

Laura   *You* don't.

Barry   What?

Laura   You don't deserve that. Nobody does.

Barry   P'raps not… I got it anyway.

       (Long pause.)

Laura   Why did you think I was like her?

Barry   *(quickly) All* women are like her. *(pause)* Least.., I thought so.

Laura   But now you're not sure?

Barry   I never met anyone like you. You got class.

Laura   Me? I'm just ordinary.

Barry   *(reacting)* No! You got class. I never met anyone with class.

Laura   I am, Barry… Ordinary… You've just never had the chance, that's all. Your mother was a bad lot, but not all women are like that.

Barry   Di's not like that.

Laura   She's brutal. She uses you.

Barry   She looks after me.

Laura   You should get away from her… Meet some ordinary people… *(pause)* I could help you.

Barry   You…? Help me…?

Laura   Yes. I could. You'd like that, wouldn't you? Just to be ordinary?

Barry   *(pensive)* Ordinary.., yeah.

Laura   *(sitting next to him)* Then let me go… Please.

Barry   I can't…! Di… *(He trails off.)*

Laura   *(desperate; pleading)* Don't you understand? She's going to kill me! I know she is.

Barry   No… she wouldn't.

Laura   She would… I can tell.

Barry   No! I won't let her!

Laura   *(impasse; after a long pause; sensing a different approach is required)* You say you respect me?

Barry   Yeah.

Laura   *(as if talking to a child)* And I respect you, Barry.

Barry   *(surprised)* You do?

Laura   Yes, of course I do. There aren't many men who would have refused me just now.

Barry   *(sullen)* You think I'm weak.

Laura   *(kneeling in front of him)* No, no I don't. A weak man would have given in. You weren't weak.

Barry   No.

Laura   A weak man would be afraid of Di, but *you're* not afraid, are you?

Barry   No. *(With bravado)* I ain't afraid of *her*.

Laura   Yet you're going to let her kill me.

Barry   I ain't! She won't hurt you! I won't let her.

Laura   How will you stop her? She's got a gun.

Barry   That!? That's a toy. It ain't real.

Laura   It's what!?

Barry   Ain't real.

Laura   You're sure?

Barry   I bought it in a toy shop. It ain't real.

Laura   So you *can* stop her?

Barry   I'll stop her. Just you see.

Laura   *(after a pause)* If I wasn't here you wouldn't *have* to stop her.

Barry   Now don't you start that again.

Laura   You don't want to be a murderer, do you?

Barry   She won't kill no-one. Not while I'm here.

Laura   But you're not always here. Sometimes you go out.

Barry   *(pensive)* Sometimes, yeah.

Laura   She couldn't hurt me if you let me go.

Barry   You'd tell the Police.

Laura   No, I wouldn't! Not if you'd helped me.

Barry   *(pause)* If I helped you... an' I were caught... would *you* help *me*?

Laura   *(sensing victory)* Yes, of course I would. I'd tell them. I'd say you let me go. *(Sensing his uncertainty; after a pause)* I would... I promise… *(tenderly)* Barry.

Barry *(reaching a decision)* All right then. I'll let you go. But I can't take you nowhere.

(Laura turns round and Barry unties her hands.)

Laura *(as he is freeing her)* That's all right, Barry. I'll find the way.

Barry Go out the back door an' across the fields towards the Church. There's a road there.

Laura *(free at last)* Thank you, Barry. I won't forget this.

Barry *(sullen)* Yeah, you will… You'll forget about me.

Laura *(moving L, then pausing before the door)* I won't… I'll remember you. I owe you my life. I can't forget that. *(She goes across to Barry and kisses him on the cheek.)*

Barry Go! Before I change my mind!

(Laura stands and goes towards the door L. As she opens it, Dianne is outside, about to enter.)

Dianne What the hell's going on?

Barry *(surprised)* Di!

(Laura tries to push Dianne out of the way and rush past, but Dianne is much too quick and too strong. Laura continues to struggle over the next few lines while Dianne brings her back in the room.)

Laura Let me go!

Dianne Not yet, my love. You get back in there. Barry, give me a hand for God's sake!

Barry *(undecided)* Leave her. Let her go.

Dianne What's the matter with you, Barry? Have you gone crazy, or something?

Barry *(she has hit a nerve)* Don't call me crazy.

Dianne Then give me a hand with this bitch!

Barry No! I've had enough, Di. I don't want no more.

(Dianne has propelled Laura next to the bed. She turns Laura to face her. Laura attempts to hit her, but Dianne parries the blow easily and her own stinging slap sends Laura sprawling face down onto the bed, where she breaks down in tears.)

Dianne Close that bloody door, Barry.

(Barry does not move.)

Close it!

(Barry rises and closes the door L. Dianne picks up the discarded rope, goes and straddles the prostrate Laura and ties her hands behind her again. She ties the rope extra tight, making Laura scream with pain.)

(Her job complete; rounding on Barry) What the hell's wrong with you? Why did you let her go?

Barry   I like her!

Dianne You *like* her!?

Barry   Yes, I like her. She's kind to me.

Dianne *(incredulous)* She's *kind* to you!? And d'you know *why* she's kind to you?

Barry   She likes me. She said so. She *respects* me.

Dianne *Respects* you!!? *(With total derision)* Hah! How could anyone respect *you*!? You're pathetic, Barry. She doesn't respect you. She wants you to let her go. She told you some sob story and you fell for it, didn't you?

Barry   *(determined)* She *said* so!

Dianne *(almost a scream)* Didn't you!?

Barry   I think we *should* let her go. She won't tell no-one. She promised.

Dianne I don't believe this! Of course she promised. She'd promise anything to get away. *(Realising)* What else did she promise?

Barry   She kissed me!

Dianne I'll bet she did. I bet she offered herself on a plate.

Barry   I didn't touch her! I said no!

Dianne Then you're even more stupid than I thought. What sort of slag offers herself to a prat like you, Barry? Have you thought about that? She's taking the piss!

Laura   *(turning to face them)* Don't listen to her, Barry. I meant it!

Dianne *(going towards Laura with a backhand raised, causing Laura to turn her head away in defence.)* Keep it shut, you! I'll sort you out later. *(Going back to Barry)* Well… have you thought about it?

Barry   *(as if it was the most important thing anyone had ever said to him)* She respects me. She said so.

Dianne You should have screwed the little slag, Barry. While she's still alive.

Barry *(rising)* Don't you touch her…

Dianne *(taunting)* Why? What will you do?

Barry Just don't touch her.

Dianne You're pathetic, Barry. *(pause)* Go and make the call.

Barry No. *You* make it. I'm not leaving you alone with her.

Dianne *(through gritted teeth)* Go and make the call, Barry.

Laura *(frantic)* Barry! Don't leave me!

Dianne *(going towards Laura; shrieking)* I told you… shut it!

Barry I'm not leaving her.

Dianne If you don't, I'll kill her now. *(She takes a knife from her belt and goes to Laura. She yanks Laura's head back and holds the knife to her throat. To Barry)* Well…?

Barry Don't! I'll go. I promise… Just don't hurt her.

Dianne *(taking the knife away and pushing Laura roughly back on the bed; softer)* That's a good boy, Barry. Don't you worry. I won't hurt your precious Laura… yet!

Barry You promise?

Dianne *(back in control of herself… and Barry)* I promise. Now off you go and make that call. I've left the words on the table.

Barry All right. I'll go. But don't hurt her.

Dianne I told you I wouldn't. Don't you trust me?

Barry *(unsure)* Well, I…

Dianne Don't you? *(pause)* 'Course you do. I've never let you down before, have I? I look after you.

Barry Yeah. I s'pose.

Dianne *(pulls Barry into an embrace and kisses him on the lips.)* Now off you go. *(Propels Barry off L, assuring him all will be well as they go. She closes the door and listens until he has gone, then goes to Laura.)*

Laura *(cowering)* Don't hurt me.

Dianne I shall have to keep an eye on you, won't I? Crafty little bitch! Thought you could wind Barry round your pretty little finger, didn't you?

Laura *(desperate)* I was only trying to… You can't blame me for that.

Dianne I don't blame you. Probably do the same thing myself. You gonna try it on me, now…? *I* would! *I* won't turn you away! *(She holds Laura's chin.)* How about it?

Laura *(twisting away)* No!

Dianne No? Later maybe. *(She throws Laura back on the bed. Suddenly hostile again)* Meanwhile… just leave Barry alone.

Laura *You* don't care about him.

Dianne Of course I don't. He's a fool.

Laura I don't know why he stays with you. You treat him like dirt.

Dianne He *is* dirt! He's trash! It's because he's such a stupid prat that he stays. He's got nothing else. You thought you were clever, didn't you, gettin' him to do what you wanted… well two can play at that game. *I* know his weaknesses, see. *(She rises and goes to the door L.)*

Laura What're you going to do?

Dianne Me? I'm going to go and have a beer. Barry's out giving dear Roger his final instructions, and tomorrow… *(trails off)*

Laura What?

Dianne Tomorrow we're going to be rich!

Laura What about me? Will you let me go?

Dianne Wait and see, my love. Wait and see.

(With an evil laugh she exits L and bolts the doors. Laura breaks down again and sobs into the bed. The lights dim stage L and come up stage R. The telephone rings, waking Roger from his sleep. He rouses unsteadily, then realises and rushes to the telephone. Carol appears in the doorway R.)

Roger *(into the receiver)* Yes…? Yes it is… *(As he talks he checks the tape is working.)* Listen, I want to speak to… What's that…? *(He motions for Carol to pick up the earphone, which she does.)* Can you say that again…?

(Roger and Carol exchange amazed glances.)

Is this some kind of joke…? Yes, yes of course, but… Is she all right…? Yes, I know where that is… Wait a minute. Let me get something to write on.

(Roger motions to Carol to get some paper and a pen from the drawer in the telephone table. She does so and hands them to him.)

Right, go on… *(He writes notes.)* Yes… At the Church… Yes…

Right, got it... What...? Yes, of course... No... No, I won't... I said I won't! Believe me, all I want is Laura... I don't care what you do, just let me have Laura back... Look, I don't know who you are, and I don't want to know, but... thanks... Ten minutes, I suppose... Yes.

(Carol and Roger put down the earphone and receiver and look at each other amazed.)

Carol   D'you think he meant it?

Roger   He sounded as though he did. Last time he phoned he had a muffled voice, as though he was trying to disguise it, but he wasn't then. And this time he sounded as though he was talking, rather than reading.

Carol   *(reaching for the phone)* We'd better tell the Inspector.

Roger   *(stopping her)* No! He said no Police.

Carol   Roger, we must. They were armed.

Roger   I don't care. He said they'd let her go, and we *have* to believe him. It's our best hope.

Carol   They might shoot you both.

Roger   I doubt it. What would they have to gain?

Carol   Nothing, I suppose. I'm just scared.

Roger   So am I, believe me. But I've got to go. I have to. If the Police call, tell them...

Carol   I'm coming with you.

Roger   No! I don't want you getting hurt.

Carol   Then I'll stay in the car, but I'm coming.

Roger   Carol..!

Carol   *(moving to the door R)* We're wasting time, Roger. Come on.

(Carol exits R. Roger is just about to exit when he remembers the tape recorder.)

Roger   Wait! *(He goes to the recorder and removes the tape.)* We don't want any nosey Police listening to that, do we?

Carol   *(off R)* Roger! Come on!

Roger   I'm coming. *(He puts a new tape in the recorder and pockets the one he has taken, then exits R.)*

(The lights dim stage R and come up stage L. The bolts on the door L are drawn back and Barry enters. Laura raises herself.)

Barry   *(holding his finger to his lips to hush her)* Don't you worry. I've told him.

Laura   *(sitting up)* What...? Who?

Barry   Your man. Roger. I've told him where you are.

Laura   Is this your idea of a joke?

Barry   No. I mean it. I told him. *(Proudly)* You respect me.

Laura   *(overcome)* Oh, Barry.

Barry   He's coming to get you. Ten minutes, he said.

Laura   But you'll be caught.

Barry   No! I said no Police.

Laura   *(concerned)* What about Di?

Barry   I'll handle her. I ain't scared of her.

Laura   You must get away from her.

Barry   She looks after me.

Laura   She doesn't care about you, Barry. You're just a means to an end for her. When she's fed up with you she'll just dump you.

Barry   I know that... But she looks after me.

Laura   Will you untie me?

Barry   Not yet. Di might come in.

Laura   You've got to get away from her. Come with us... we'll take you into town.

Barry   No! There's Police in town. They'll hurt me. Di says so.

Laura   Then we'll take you somewhere... Anywhere away from her.

(There is a noise off L.)

Barry   Quick. It's Di. Don't say nothing.

(Laura sinks back on the bed. Barry moves guiltily away. Dianne enters L. She notices the atmosphere and looks suspiciously between Laura and Barry.)

Dianne What's been happening..? Barry...

Barry   Nothing's been happening. We was talking.

Dianne *(moves to Laura)* Have you been winding him up again? *(Checks Laura's bonds.)*

Laura   No. As he said, we were talking.

Dianne What about?

Barry   Er… Police! We was talking about Police!

Laura   *(quickly)* Yes, that's right. He was saying he didn't like them.

Dianne That's right, Barry, my love. We don't like the Police. That's because if they catch us they'll lock us up, and we know what'll happen then, don't we?

Barry   *(uneasy)* Yeah.

Dianne Just remember that, Barry, before you do anything else stupid. They'd love you in prison. They'd make fun of you, Barry. They *love* fools.

Barry   I *ain't* a fool!

Dianne Not to mention what else they'd do. No women, you see, Barry, so someone has to keep them amused. They'd really *love* you! *(She laughs mockingly.)* You'd *never* be able to sit down.

Roger   *(off L; distant; calling)* Hello…! Laura..!

Dianne *(wheeling round)* What the…? Shit, Barry, what have you done?

Barry   *(defiant)* I *told* him.

Dianne You what!?

Laura   *(calling)* Roger! Up here!

Roger   *(off L; distant; calling)* Laura..!?

Dianne *(pulling the gun from her belt and aiming at Laura)* Shut it!

Laura   You don't frighten me with that. I know it's not real.

Dianne *(berating him)* You stupid bastard, Barry..! You've really cocked it up this time, haven't you? *(She thrusts the gun at him.)* Here, hold this on her. Hubby doesn't know it's not real… Unless you told him that as well?

Barry   No, I…

Dianne Then hold it! Barry, do as I say!

Laura   Roger..!

(Dianne slaps Laura back onto the bed. She pulls out her knife, goes behind Laura and puts one hand across her mouth. She pulls the knife out of her belt and holds it across Laura's throat. They look towards the door and wait for Roger.)

Dianne Not a *word*, you bitch!

Roger   *(close to the door)* Laura? Where are you?

(Laura tries to speak but only a moan can be heard.)

Dianne *(calling)* In here, Roger.

(The door L opens and Roger enters. Barry points the gun towards him. He sees Laura and starts to make a dart towards them, but halts when he notices the gun.)

That's far enough.

Roger   *(holding his hands out to stop them)* All right! I'm unarmed. There's no Police. I just want Laura.

Dianne   Yes, I'm sure you do, my love. But you can't have her. You see, there's been a change of plan.

Roger   But the man said that I could...

Dianne   I know what he said... but she isn't his to give back.

Roger   Laura, are you O.K? *(Laura tries to speak, but cannot.)* Let her speak, for God's sake! What harm can it do?

(After a moment of consideration Dianne takes her hand from Laura's mouth.)

Laura   *(quickly)* Roger... the gun... it's a fake.

(Roger is about to make a lunge for Barry.)

Dianne   *(tightening her grip on Laura and holding the knife closer to her throat)* But this knife ain't! Another step and I'll cut her throat!

Roger   *(stopping dead)* All right, all right! Don't do anything stupid!

Barry   *(reacting)* I ain't stupid.

Roger   *(recognising Barry's voice)* It was you I spoke to on the phone, wasn't it? You said you'd let me take her.

Barry   That's right.

Dianne   Except you can't take her. Just because Barry's stupid enough to fall for her lies doesn't mean I am. This doesn't change anything.

Barry   *(insistent)* I *ain't* stupid!

Dianne   Piss off, Barry! Ain't you done enough damage for one day!?

Roger   Just let us go.

Laura   Please!

Dianne   No! You've got work to do. The wages, remember?

Roger   I'll still do it. Just let us go. We'll do anything you say.

Dianne   You must think I'm as stupid as *he* is! No, we'll have to change our plans a bit, but the job goes ahead.

Roger   I'm not leaving without her.

Laura   Roger, no! Don't upset her!

Dianne That's right, Roger. Don't upset me. *(to Laura)* I get nasty when I'm upset, don't I, my love? *(She tightens her grip on Laura. With menace)* Don't I?

Laura *(afraid)* Yes, yes!

(Roger takes a step towards them.)

Dianne *(holding Laura's head up so he can see the knife)* Get back! *(Roger stops.)* That's better. Now sit over there. *(She indicates the chair. Roger does not move.)* Sit! *(Roger goes to the chair and sits.)* We've been having a nice time, Laura and me. *(As she talks she starts to caress Laura's body to taunt him, still holding the knife close to her throat.)* We've become good friends, haven't we, Laura? *(She moves the knife and cuts off the top button of Laura's blouse.)* Very good friends!

Roger *(rising)* You hurt her and…

Dianne *(reacting)* Get back or I'll cut her throat!

(Roger resumes his seat.)

(taunting) You'll *what* Roger? What will you do?

Roger *(calmly and coldly)* You hurt her and I swear I'll kill you.

Dianne *(amused; sarcastic)* I'm terrified, my love. Absolutely trembling with fear! *(with venom)* It ain't easy killing someone. Specially the first time… *I* know.

Roger What d'you want from us?

Dianne I told you… same as before. Now, thanks to this thick bastard we'll have to move out of this place, of course. And *you'll* have to get rid of the Police. I assume they're outside somewhere?

Roger No! The Police don't know I'm here.

Barry I don't like Police. They hurt me.

Roger I'll do anything you say. Just don't hurt her.

Laura They're not going to let me go, Roger. I know it.

Dianne How can you say that, my love? We've treated you well, haven't we? *(The threat again)* Haven't we!?

Laura Yes! Ow, you're hurting me.

Dianne Whether we let you go or not depends on you. Do as we say and we let you get on with your lives. Cross us at all and… *(The rest is left unsaid.)*

Roger How do I know we can trust you?

Dianne You don't. You'll just have to take my word for it.

Barry   We won't hurt her. She respects me.

         (Roger looks curiously at Barry.)

Dianne   *(amused)* There you are! Even Barry says she'll be all right. And if he says it it *must* be true. *(With venom)* He's too bloody stupid to lie convincingly!

Barry   *(angry; taking a step towards her; his gun raised)* Don't call me stupid! I *ain't* stupid!

Dianne   Sit down, Barry!

         (Barry slowly points the gun at Dianne and pulls the trigger. There is a dull click.)

         (Amused) It's a *toy*, Barry. Remember?

Barry   *(looking curiously at the gun)* Toy.

Roger   *(resigned)* What d'you want me to do?

Dianne   Laura here will stay as our guest, won't you, my love? Like I said, we've become good friends, Laura and me. You go back home as if nothing's changed. Except we want you to *bring* us the money.

Roger   But you said I just had to…

Dianne   I know what we said. That was just a story to keep the local pigs happy. You get the money and we'll let you know where to take it. When *we* get the money, *you* get Laura. Simple, ain't it? But you tell the Police any of this and I cut Laura up into little pieces and send her back bit by bit. And make sure the police don't follow, 'cause we'll be watching every move you make. Got it?

Roger   *(resigned)* Yes.

Laura   Can I have a few minutes alone with Roger?

Dianne   Oh, no. If you'd behaved yourselves and done like we said, then maybe. But we've been naughty boys and girls, haven't we? So no kisses and cuddles.

Barry   *(still looking at the gun)* Toy.

         (More noises off L.)

Dianne   *(tightening her grip on Laura and moving the knife back to her throat)* What's that!? If you brought someone else…

Barry   No Police! I said no Police!

Roger   I didn't! I swear! It's probably Carol. I told her to stay in the car.

Dianne   *(hushed)* Everyone quiet! Not a word!

         (After a few moments the door bursts open and Dave enters. He

holds a raised pistol which he aims at Barry. Maria is close behind him.)

Dave Police! Put down your weapon or I fire!

Barry *(as they enter)* No Police! *(He raises the toy gun.)*

Dave Put the gun down!

Barry *(the gun raised)* Toy!

(Barry pulls the trigger to demonstrate. Dave quickly fires a shot and Barry is thrown backwards as he is hit. He slumps to the floor and after a few convulsions lies inert.)

Laura *(as Barry falls; screaming; she tries to rise but Dianne holds her)* No! *(collapsing back; overcome)* No…! It was a toy!

Dianne *(pulling Laura to a standing position and standing behind her, the knife close at her throat)* But this ain't

(Dave raises the gun and points at them.)

Roger *(rising)* No! Don't shoot! You'll hit Laura!

Maria *(calming)* Put the knife down, Miss. It's all over.

Dianne That's just where you're wrong. *You* put the *gun* down, *pig*. Better still, give it to me.

Dave *(still pointing the gun)* You know I can't do that.

Dianne Then she dies!

Roger No!

Maria Now calm down. We've had one shooting. We don't want any more.

Dianne Then give me the gun!

Maria No! There's no way we'll give you that gun. You must know that. *(There are a few moments impasse. To Dave)* Sergeant, lower your weapon.

Dave *(still pointing his gun)* But Ma'am, we can't…

Maria *(firmly)* Lower your weapon, Sergeant!

Dave Against regulations, Ma'am.

Laura For God's sake…!

Maria Sod regulations! Do it!

(Dave lowers the gun reluctantly.)

Maria Now, put it on the table over there.

Dave What!?

Maria   Just do it…! *Now!*

       (Dave reluctantly does as instructed.)

       Now, Miss… How about letting Mrs Nuttall go?

Dianne   You must think I'm stupid.

Laura   For God's sake, Dianne! Barry might be dying!

Dianne   Serves him right! He would've shot *me* if that gun'd been a real one. Stupid bastard!

Maria   Don't make the same mistake he did. Let her go and we can talk.

Dianne   No way. I'm getting out of here. And *she's* coming with me.

Roger   No, please. Haven't you done enough?

Dianne   I'm not doing time for no-one.

       (Dianne starts towards the door L, holding Laura in front of her as a shield.)

       Come on! Out of my way.

Dave   *(starting towards them)* Give it up. You can't get away.

Dianne   Get back!

Maria   Do as she says, Sergeant!

Dianne   *(to Maria)* Give me your keys! Come on, you cow! Your car keys… now!

       (Maria reaches in her pocket, takes out a bunch of keys and hands them to Dianne. As she takes them, Maria suddenly grabs the hand which is holding the knife and a struggle ensues. Laura struggles free and runs into the arms of Roger, who puts himself in a position to shield her from any possible injury. Maria is strong enough to force Dianne's knife away from her, but in the fight the knife catches her stomach and a large bloodstain appears on her.)

       Get off me, you bitch!

Maria   Sergeant! Get the knife.

       (Dave takes hold of Dianne's hand and roughly forces the knife from it, then takes charge of her. Maria takes handcuffs from her bag and handcuffs Dianne's hands behind her.)

Dianne   Pigs!

Dave   Now, that's not very polite, is it?

Maria   *(she puts her hand to her wound.)* Take her to the car, Sergeant.

Call an ambulance.

Dave   Yes, Ma'am. *(He takes Dianne towards the door L. He notices Maria has been injured.)* You all right, Ma'am…?

Maria   I'll survive.

Dave   And, er… Ma'am…

Maria   *(coldly; expecting criticism)* What is it, Sergeant?

Dave   Good job done, Ma'am.

(Maria looks amazed as Dave and Dianne exit L. Roger is untying Laura's hands.)

Maria   You all right, Mrs Nuttall?

Laura   Yes, I'm O.K. *(Indicating Barry)* What about…?

Maria   *(checks Barry's pulse and eyes.)* I'm afraid not.

Laura   *(into Roger's shoulder)* Oh, God! He tried to help me. He tried to protect me from *her*.

Roger   I know. He phoned me and told me where to find you.

Laura   *(rounding on Maria)* It was a toy gun, for God's sake. Why did you have to kill him!? *(Sobs into Roger's shoulder.)*

Maria   We had no way of knowing, Mrs Nuttall. Sergeant Robinson was reacting to what he saw. It's all he could do.

Roger   I don't understand… How did you find us? How did you know?

Maria   A combination of luck and opportunity. The man - Barry - stayed on the telephone long enough for us to complete the trace. We'd come to the area to ask the locals if they'd seen any newcomers when the call came through. He'd used the callbox near the local shop. He was gone when we arrived, but as we were driving away we spotted your car in the lane. Very distinctive, that car. Mrs Anderson told us what had happened.

Roger   They were going to take Laura away again.

Maria   It's just as well we spotted you. We've been searching the computer looking for similar cases. If they're the ones we think they are this would have been their fourth similar job.

Laura   The other jobs… did the wife..?

Maria   No, Mrs Nuttall. It's as well we found you when we did.

Laura   I can't believe it! *(Looks at Barry)* He acted tough… but I would never have thought…

Maria   In all probability it wasn't him, Ma'am. Our evidence suggests that it was the same woman with another man. Previous descriptions fit her exactly, but the man had red hair.

Laura Then Barry wasn't involved?

Maria We can't be absolutely sure, but I'd say not. We found a red-haired man not far from where the last wife was found. He'd been stabbed. He died without regaining consciousness.

Roger *(hugs Laura)* Thank God we found you in time. It's been a nightmare. I still can't believe it's over. *(Referring to Maria's injury)* Are you all right, Inspector?

Maria Yes, it looks worse than it is. I'll go in the ambulance and have it seen to.

Roger Occupational hazard, eh?

Maria My God, I hope not. It hurts like hell. I'll be O.K. You take your wife home.

Roger We can go?

Maria Yes, sir. We'll finish up here and come and see you later. We'll need a statement.

Roger Right, Inspector… And thank you. Look… I'm sorry I didn't call you, but they said no Police, and…

Maria Yes, sir. I *do* understand. I wonder what I'd have done in the same circumstances… Still, life must go on. Just go home and forget it all happened. This way. *(Exits)*

Laura *(goes to Barry)* No, we'll never be able to do that. Life may go on for us, but… *(Touches his cheek tenderly, shakes her head ruefully.)*

Roger Come on. *(Supports Laura as he leads her off L. The CURTAIN slowly falls.)*

Properties

Stage Layout

On stage:-

    Settee *(c)*

    Matching armchair *(R)*

    Dining chair *(above C)*

    Small telephone table *(Above R)*

        In it: paper

                pen

        On it: modern telephone

                directories

    Television set *(Down R)*

    Radio cassette player *(on shelf)*

Dirty old bed (or straw bales and blanket) *(Up LC)*
Table *(L)*
Single chair *(L)*
TV remote control *(Laura)*
Personal:-
    Blue suit jacket *(Roger - Off R)*
    Blue tie *(Roger - Off R)*
    Wristwatch *(Roger)*
    Two mugs of coffee *(Laura - Off R)*
    Wristwatch *(Laura)*
    Shoulder bag *(Dianne - Off R)*
        In it: Small bottle of liquid
                        Cotton wool pad
                        Pistol
                        Two ski masks
    Ties, etc. *(Barry - Off R + one worn)*
    Notebook *(Dave - in his pocket)*
    Pen *(Dave - in his pocket)*
    Glass of whisky *(Roger - Off R)*
    Plastic carrier bag *(Barry - Off R)*
        In it: Container of curry
                        Container of fried rice
                        Container of sweet and sour
                        Bag of chips
                        Plastic spoons
    Cassette recorder *(Dave - Off R)*
    Earpiece *(Dave - Off R)*
    Electronic box *(Dave - Off R)*
    Wires *(Dave - Off R)*
    Box of cassette tapes *(Dave - Off R)*
    Watch *(Dave)*
    Framed photograph of Laura *(Maria - off R)*
    Business card *(Maria - in her pocket)*
    Instant camera *(Barry - Off L)*
    Small tape recorder *(Barry - Off L)*
    Slip of paper *(Dianne - Off L)*
    Cup of coffee *(Dianne - Off L)*
    Tray of cups, etc. *(Carol - Off R)*
    Coffee pot *(Carol - Off R)*
    Two letters *(Carol - Off R)*
    Small package *(Carol - Off R)*
        In it: Cassette tape
                        Typewritten note

Black document case *(Maria - Off R)*
    In it: Multi-page typed document
                Polythene gloves
                Plastic bags
Two mugs of tea *(Barry - Off L)*
Knife *(Dianne - in her belt)*
Pistol *(Dave - Off L)*
Shoulder bag (Maria)
    In it: Bunch of keys
                Handcuffs

AUTHOR'S NOTES

"The Price to Pay" is not a story about a robbery or a kidnap so much as how the situation affects those involved. The subject matter, the violence, the sexual undertones and (if used) the strong language may put some societies off. It is worth remembering, however, that this is essentially a moral play. Good finally triumphs over evil, but there is a price to pay.

The split set is very easy to achieve - the simplest method is to decorate the "house" half and paint the "barn" side black. Dividing walls are not necessary. After early performances both audience and players had no problems accepting the existence of the two playing areas.

The play's start is deliberately light and gentle so as to achieve the full impact of the intrusion into the couple's lives. The barn where Laura is taken should be as hostile as possible. Black-painted walls are entirely appropriate. The sense of isolation when she awakes can prove very powerful and emphasised by her despair at being unable to escape.

As the play proceeds we have a shift of power until Laura - a fairly weak personality at the start, compromises herself out of desperation until she is able to exercise some control over Barry, and is the cause of his eventual destruction. Dianne, ruthlessly and callously in control of Barry for most of the play, eventually loses that control by her brutal treatment of something Barry has never experienced before - someone who, on the surface at least, is gentle and caring. Barry starts brutal and hostile, but this is a façade resulting from Dianne's total influence over him. When he rejects Laura's eventual advances to him he is not pushing her away, he is pushing his mother away. He does not want this apparently gentle woman to be like her. He gradually loses his violence as Dianne's hold over him diminishes, and with it he also loses his grip on his sanity. The swing in Barry's character is demonstrated by the contrast between the episode in ACT I where he brutally assaults Laura and the episode in ACT II where she tries to seduce him - a gentle, almost sympathetic scene.

At one production of this play the final curtain was delayed for some time leaving Barry alone on the stage - a sad, lonely character who died alone and unloved, having perished for the one glimpse of purity he had ever experienced.

Great play can also be made of the "moonlight" scene - but with care. Overplaying this scene (immediately before the interval) can make it over-sentimental or even comic. Roger and Laura may be on stage together, but the emphasis must be on how alone they are. Some silence, then subtle music and lighting, plus the cold light of the moon, can turn this scene into a powerful tear-jerker.

Dianne is a contrast in herself. At times brutal, at times maternal, she cares for nobody but herself. With careful playing we need not be sure until the end whether she had actually killed before, whether she does indeed have lesbian tendencies or whether that was just another way to emphasise her sadistic power over Laura.

We are also left during the play with the possibility that Carol is in some way implicated, or perhaps even her husband. Both of these have been picked up by early performances of the play, as was the possibility that Dave may also be a "villain".

The interplay between the police provides a nice sub-plot. Dave despises Maria and is quite prepared to sacrifice Laura to get her removed. Played correctly we should realise at the end that - while Maria has triumphed, this is just an episode - he will try again.

As with all good theatre, the aim is to leave the audience wanting more. There is the opportunity with this play to do that. For example, they should not be entirely comfortable that Barry died, that Dianne survived, that "nice" Roger was probably sincere with his threat that he would kill to rescue her or that "nice" Laura was prepared to sacrifice *anything* to escape. We can be left with the question as to how much sympathy and affection she actually developed for the character, and - most importantly - how the couple's lives have been affected.

We should have seen the characters' personalities become closer - Roger, Laura, Carol and Maria gaining life experience and having to become harder and tougher to cope - Barry and Dave mellowing because of the people who have touched their lives. Finally Dianne - as sadistic at the end as at the start.

Other plays by Ian Hornby - see www.scripts4theatre.com

Abanazar's Revenge	Jayne with a Y
Aladdin dot com	Late of This Address
'Allo, 'Allo, 'Allo, (Est There Any Body La)?	Mind Games
Are You Sure There's No Body There?	Murdered, Presumed Dead
Be Careful Who You Wish For	No, Minister
Boomerang	One Across
The Cat's Away	The Price to Pay
Cinderella	A Question of Innocence
Cold Blood	Remember Me
Conference Pairs	Robin Hood
The Dark Side of the Son	Shades of Blue
D I Why?	Situation Vacant
A Dish Served Cold	Tied Up at the Office
Do You Keep Stationery?	To Sleep, Perchance
Dream, Lover!	Voices
The Ex Factor	Wait Until the Ghost is Clear
An Eye for an Eye, Darling	Where There's a Will...
Hello, Is There Any Body There?	Whispers
Help! I'm a Celebrity Pantomime Dame; Get Me Out of Here!	Whose Line Was It, Anyway?
The Hex Factor	Why Won't They Believe Me?
Jack Up!	The Winter of Discontent